Sugar Coated Love

JOY AVERY

SUGAR COATED LOVE

First Print Edition: March 2020

ISBN: 9798621222468

DEDICATION

Dedicated to the dream.

DEAR READER,

As always, THANK YOU for your support of #joyaveryromance. I am overwhelmed by your dedication and support. I'm also highly grateful. You will never know how much I appreciate you, but I'll try to show you by continuing to bring you beautiful love stories.

One reason why I loved penning Finley and Cash's love journey is because I got to explore a place I love, Chicago. I hope you enjoy reading this friends-to-lovers tale as much as I enjoyed writing it.

Please help me spread the word about SUGAR COATED LOVE by recommending it to friends and family, book clubs, social media, and online forums. I'd also like to ask that you take a moment to leave a review on the site where you purchased this book. Reviews help to keep our love stories alive!

I love hearing from readers. Feel free to email me: authorjoyavery@gmail.com

Wishing you light, love, and happy reading!

P.S.: Be sure to check out the other books in the Carnivale Chronicles series.

ACKNOWLEDGMENTS

My thanks—first and foremost—to God for blessing me with this gift of storytelling.

To anyone who has ever guided me in any way on this beautiful journey, I acknowledge you!

CHAPTER 1

Finley Cooper groaned at the sound of her chiming office phone. Had it not been for the fact she was expecting a call from Mr. Kilmer, her favorite client, she would have simply allowed it to roll into voicemail. All she needed was another strike on her record for being late to a staff meeting, especially another so close to the last she'd gotten a few days ago for overstepping her boss in a meeting with a potential client.

One thing you didn't do was outshine Madison L. VanBeran, especially at her own advertising agency. The stern woman was proof the devil not only wore Prada, but also Saint Laurent, guzzled a gallon of dark roast an hour and barked orders like a drill sergeant. Apparently, such a strategy worked for her, because her agency was the one every successful or wanted-to-be successful business sought out.

The death stare Madison had given her that day in the meeting still made her shiver from the mere frost of it. But in Finley's defense, she was genuinely attempting to help. It hadn't felt as if Madison was grasping the vision being presented to her. In Finley's opinion, Madison had offered the millennial clients baby boomer ideas.

Rounding her desk again, Finley answered the line. Sure enough Mr. Kilmer's deep voice boomed over the line. After a quick greeting, he preceded to inform her of how much he'd loved the proposal for his company's new line of aftershave products, and how it appealed to an age demographic he'd never even considered.

While Finley had a great deal of admiration and respect for Mr. Kilmer—the man who'd taken a chance on the still-wet-behind-the-ears newbie ten years ago—like her boss, he sometimes didn't see the greater potential of a campaign. Luckily, he had her.

After a brief update on a few minor changes Finley proposed for the graphic layout, she ended the call with Mr. Kilmer, snatched up her things and hurried for the conference room. As expected, she was the last to arrive, drawing attention as she rushed through the door.

"*Miss* Cooper." Madison's voice boomed through the room. "So thrilled you could join us this morning. Five minutes late, but at least you're here, right?"

At sixty-ish, Madison was in better shape than most twenty year olds. The short pixie cut made her look younger than her true age, though the full head of silver hair revealed her maturity. With her flawless, mahogany-toned complexion and modelesque physique she could still—and often times did—turn heads. If only her inner beauty mirrored her outer beauty.

"I apologize," Finley said, taking her seat around the populated conference table. "I had to take a last-minute call from Mr. Kilmer."

It was slight, but Finley noticed the grimace on Madison's face at the mention of Mr. Kilmer's name. Madison had gifted Mr. Kilmer's account to Finley when she'd first started. Later Finley learned it had been because the woman hadn't felt the mediocre (Madison's exact words) company had been worth her time or energy. As the newbie, Finley had gushed over the opportunity to work with the black-owned startup, now valued at close to a billion dollars and one of M. VanBeran's top clients.

Things had soured between Madison and Mr. Kilmer when he'd objected to Madison's attempt to reclaim his account and all but demanded Finley continue as the lead. If Finley had to guess, it had been the first time a man had ever denied Madison VanBeran anything. Clearly, the woman still held a grudge, but being an astute business woman, who recognized the value in keeping Mr. Kilmer happy, she'd abided by his wishes.

Madison cupped her hands together and forced a smile that seemed almost painful for her to display.

"Yes, dear, we must keep Mr. Kilmer happy." She stood, ironed a hand down the front of the expensive-looking midnight blue dress she wore and strolled the length of the room, her sparkling heels clacking against the wood floor.

For several long and intense minutes, Madison's attention remained through the wall of floor-to-ceiling windows that gave a breathtaking view of downtown Raleigh. This silent stroll usually signaled trouble. The twenty or so people eyed one another, perhaps attempting to figure out who would be the recipient of Madison's tirade this week. Finley breathed a sigh of relief when she considered the fact that she was safe. Since her last run-in with Madison, she'd managed to keep her nose squeaky clean.

"*Miss* Cooper?"

Finley tensed at the sound of her name. At least she'd thought she'd kept her nose squeaky clean. "Y-yes." Finley loathed how weak she'd sounded.

Madison continued, "Please give me one great reason why I shouldn't fire you."

Fire her? What had she done to warrant being terminated? Finley's eyes swept the table, most everyone dropping their gazes as if to avoid being found guilty by association. Or did they know something she didn't know? Facing Madison, she said, "I'm not sure I follow."

"I, too, received a last-minute telephone call. Only mine was from Teakwood."

Instantly, Finley recognized the name as being the company she and Madison had met with a week prior. A knot tightened in her stomach. Madison moved back to her seat, but didn't sit. Instead, she rested her folded arms across the top of the maroon-colored leather chair—resembling a downsized throne—and stared at Finley for several uncomfortable seconds.

"Would you like to guess why they were

phoning?" Madison asked.

Finley slumped a little in her chair, having a pretty good idea already. "Um—"

Madison cut her off before she could finish her thought. "I'll tell you why. To inform me that The M. VanBeran Agency was no longer being considered."

Finley gnawed the inside of her jaw unsure how, or if, she should even bother to respond. No need to make the situation worse than it already was. If that were even possible. Was Madison serious about firing her? She'd dedicated ten years to the company. That had to stand for something, right? It wasn't like she'd intentionally set out to tank a deal with a prospective client.

Finley could feel every set of eyes in the room beaming at her. The large space felt no bigger than a sardine can, and was just as suffocating. The conversation would have been better had in private; unfortunately, public shaming was Madison's thing.

For the next several minutes, Madison berated her like a child in front of her colleagues. It would have been embarrassing had every single person at the table had not fallen victim to one of Madison's blowups at one time or another. Still, it wasn't cool.

"Well, do you have anything to say for

yourself, or are you just going to sit there like a rooster on a fence?" Madison asked.

Cock-a-doodle-doo. Of course, Finley kept that too herself. Again, all eyes were on Finley in obvious anticipation of her response. Yes, she was going to say something. Something she should have said a long time ago. Something that this evil hen of a woman needed to hear. "I—"

"Moving on," Madison snapped, flashing Finley a look of disgust.

Finley shrank in her chair, feeling smaller than the tip of a sewing needle. And pissed that she lacked the backbone to exert her voice. Weren't the stacks of self-help books on her nightstand supposed to have made her more assertive? Along with the motivational audiobooks she frequently listened to on her drives into the office? Weren't they supposed to give her the courage it took to stand up to her domineering boss and demand change? Respect?

I deserve respect, dammit!

Her head lifted a little higher.

I don't deserve to be spoken to like an animal in the street.

She sat a little straighter.

I am worthy.

Finley squared her shoulders and bolted

from her seat, the force of the action sending the chair clattering backwards and startling herself, along with several others, if their gasps were any indication. Recovering quickly, she said. "Yes, I do have something to say."

Madison rolled her eyes heavenward as if whatever Finley had to say would be a waste of her time. Off a heavy sigh, she said, "Well, spit it out then. We don't have all day."

Finley prepared herself to tick off all of the things that swirled around in her head, but when she opened her mouth, the words "I quit," flew out.

*

Cassius "Cash" Warren rang up the last customer in the line, signaling the end of their breakfast rush. People would trickle in from now until noon, when Pleasure Pastries would swell once again with hungry patrons. While he had a limited lunch menu, folks seemed to enjoy the offerings. He hoped to, in the coming months, expand his menu to include even more options. But right now, slow and steady was the key.

He was proud of the work he'd done with the shop after inheriting it from his late-sister nearly two years prior. In that time, he'd turned the struggling business into a local treasure, while keeping his sister's vision intact. But he hadn't done it alone.

As his thoughts of Finley materialized, the woman miraculously strolled through the door as if he'd summoned her. This wasn't her usual time to visit. Normally, she showed up at lunchtime, then again on her way home.

Tiny spiral curls in her hair bounced with each step she took, along with her full breasts. The ones he fantasized about cupping, licking, sucking far more times than he cared to admit. The curve-hugging dress she wore highlighted her perfectly-proportioned body. He had no doubt she would feel amazing under him. Something rumbled in his chest. Desire? No, pure need.

After chatting with his father and uncle briefly, then tossing her hand up at him, Finley ventured to the table in the back of the shop where she always sat.

Something felt off with her. The brilliant smile that usually lit the space when she entered—and heated his chest just a little— okay, a lot, if he was being a hundred percent honest—was absent, replaced by a dull gleam. This wasn't the Finley he was used too.

Her boss strikes again, if he had to guess. For the life of him, he couldn't understand why

11

Finley stayed at a company lead by a maniac. With her talent, she could easily start her own branding and advertising agency. It would undoubtedly be a success. She brought life to everything she touched. Or brought life back, in his case.

Eldridge Warren, Cash's father, clapped him on the shoulder from behind. "Uh-oh. Looks like someone needs some cheering up, and there's only one person in this city who can do that. So, go 'head. I've got the counter."

Cash eyed his father. They stood nearly shoulder to shoulder in height, but Cash held about an half inch advantage. Still in decent shape for his age, the retired postmaster often helped him around the shop. Precision trimmed salt and pepper hair and beard made him look distinguished.

"Old man, why do you have to always place hidden innuendo in your words when it comes to Finley. Like I've said a hundred times before, we're just friends."

For some reason that title didn't quite seem to fit what they were. No, they weren't having sex, never had, but what they shared felt like far more than just a simple friendship. She'd helped him cope with losing his sister and only sibling, had been there for him when his fiancée had decided she wasn't cut out to be a caregiver after he'd been burned in an accident, had made him laugh when he'd preferred to have been livid with the world instead.

So, yeah, he had a soft spot in his heart for his late-sister's best friend. The problem was, it was softer than it should have been. Despite how he felt about Finley, he wouldn't cross that line. Not with her. She meant too much to him to jeopardize their bond.

"Son, do I look blind to you? Whenever Finley comes around, you light up like a kid at Christmas. I don't get why you're so afraid to unwrap such a beautiful present."

"Because he's scared. That's how they making them these days. Scaredy cats."

Cash slid his gaze over to his father's brother, Rudolph Warren. The man was almost an identical copy of his older brother. The most noticeable difference were their complexions. Like Cash's, Eldridge's skin tone was a creamy dark chocolate, while Rudolph's was a slight shade lighter.

Rudolph occupied his usual seat at the only booth inside the establishment. While the gold piece of furniture stood out like an elephant in a henhouse amongst the vivid yellows, browns and greens, Cash couldn't imagine getting rid of it. His father and Rudolph were like kings when they sat there, and it symbolized to everyone who entered just how important they were. Plus, it had been Jaicee's favorite piece.

He smiled at the thought of his baby sister, then ached thinking about the circumstances surrounding her death. Not a day flew by he didn't miss her or didn't blame himself for her absence. Pushing the pain aside, he eyed his uncle. "Will you please keep your voice down? And scared?" Cash laughed. "Whatever, old man number two."

"Things were different in our day. When we saw a woman we liked, we told her straight up how we felt. That's how we got the girl. We didn't play no cat and mouse games. How you think your daddy got your momma. Back me up, Ridge," Rudolph said, addressing Eldridge by the nickname he'd used for as long as Cash could remember.

Cash glanced toward his father, who nodded his agreement. He didn't bother trying to explain to them *again* that he and Finley were just friends.

"She's clearly waiting for you to make the first move, son, but no woman will wait forever," his father said. "You should invite her with you to Chicago. Make it a road trip. Take in the sights along the way. You'd be amazed what could happen in close quarters."

Cash sighed. "You two need something

better to do than to try and orchestrate my love life."

"What love life?" his father and Rudolph said in unison, then burst into laughter.

"Keep on and I'm gonna have you both committed. I'll call the authorities and say there are two crazy old men loitering in my shop and talking out of their heads."

Rudolph grinned. "Have me committed. The crazy house is the second-best place to meet women."

Cash shook his head. "I'm fairly certain the term crazy house is politically incorrect, Uncle Rudolph."

"Who gon' do something 'bout it? Send them my way. I'll beat 'em like Ali did Foreman. That Ali." Rudolph slapped the table. "The greatest of all times. Now that was one dynamic man. You know that's why your father named you Cassius. He took one look into your eyes and said he saw the strength and determination of a warrior in them."

Cash eyed his father again. The man donned a look of pride that made Cash's heart swell. Until now, he'd assumed his father had simply named him after his favorite boxer.

"You know where the first best place to meet woman is?" Rudolph asked.

"I'm afraid to ask, but out of curiosity,"

Cash said, "where?"

"The old folks home. I keep trying to get your cousin to put me in one, but she's afraid I'll get all those hot things in there pregnant. You know I still got it, right?"

"I'm leaving now," Cash said, moving away from the two laughing men.

Cash grabbed a fresh baked orange and cranberry muffin—Finley's favorite—before heading to join her as he did most days. Approaching the table, he slid the dessert plate in front of her. "Looks like you could use this."

When she glanced up at him, his heart skipped a beat. God, she was beautiful. Innocent brown eyes, a cute button nose, soft-looking, kissable lips, and flawless brown skin. Brown hair with warm red and golden undertones framed her heart-shaped face. He could stare at her forever.

"I'm not very hungry right now," she said.

Finley's voice snapped him from his stupor, and he eased down into the chair across from her. Despite her claim, she pulled the plate closer to her, pinched off a piece and popped it into her mouth. She closed her eyes and hummed her apparent satisfaction. The gentle sound produced an inappropriate visual of Finley lying beneath him in his bed.

Refocusing, he said, "Wanna tell me what's

16

wrong, or should I guess?"

She claimed another piece of the muffin. "Oh, you'd never guess this in a hundred years."

"You quit your job?" he said with a chuckle. When Finley stopped mid chew and eyed him quizzically, his brows furrowed. "Wait, did you quit your job?"

She nodded.

"That's great, Fin. Congratulations! I'm proud of you."

Finley pushed the plate away. "Don't applaud my stupidity," she said. "God, what have I done?"

Well, color him confused because it sounded as if she regretted her decision.

"Do you know how many people would lie, cheat, and steal for an opportunity to work at M. VanBeran?"

Cash shrugged. "I—"

"*Hundreds*," she said, cutting him off. "That's how many resumes arrive in the office a month. Hundreds. If you're in advertising, M. VanBeran is the place you want to be. And in one idiotic moment, I tossed it all away." She buried her face in her hands. "What am I going to do now?"

*

A shock of heat rushed through Finley when Cash peeled her hands away from her face and held them firm inside his. She loved the way his big, warm hands felt nestled against hers. Studying their intertwined fingers, she willed herself to ignore the butterflies thrashing in her stomach. While she could try to deny the effect he had on her body, she couldn't deny the effect he had on her heart.

Nope, there was no denying the fact that she had feelings for him. And boy had she tried. From the very moment her best friend had introduced him as her *big-headed* older brother. Six years ago. If this man had any idea how she felt about him, he'd probably run, which was reason alone not to tell him. She'd grown accustomed to having him in her life.

Bringing her gaze up to meet his, his tranquil brown eyes soothed her. It was strange how he'd always had such an effect on her. Normally, she avoided holding a connection with him like this for too long, in fear of him seeing something in her eyes that would reveal her feelings. But for some reason, this time she couldn't look away.

"You know what you're going to do, Finley Rosette Cooper? You're going to do what you've always wanted to do and start your own agency."

Starting her own agency had been something she'd talked about for forever. But it had been just that, talk. Maybe ten years ago it would have been feasible, but she was thirty-two now. It would take at least five years, if not more, to establish herself as a real player in the branding and advertising game. And even then, there was no guarantee of success. And what if Madison retaliated and blackballed her? What would she do then? She'd be jobless and broke.

"Maybe I still have time to call Madison, do a bit of groveling to get my job back," she said.

"I won't let you do it," Cash said. "You're not just good at what you do, Finley, you're great. So, why not use your steam to fuel your own dream instead of someone else's? In no time you'll have people asking M. VanBeran, who?"

Cash smiled and two deep dimples pierced his smooth, dark brown skin. Like always, she wanted to reach over and touch the indentations. And like always, she was forced to resist.

She eyed him several beats, considering his words before finally saying, "Maybe I can convince Madison I was on strong medicine and was unaware of what I was saying."

Cash tossed his head back and groaned.

"Finley. You can do this."

"How are you so convinced?" she asked.

Without skipping a beat, he said, "Because I believe in you. Now you just have to believe in yourself."

She stared at him, touched by his words. While she should have been focused on her dire situation, all she wanted to do was straddle Cash's lap and glide her tongue along his bobbing Adam's apple. How would his stubble feel against her skin as she kissed her way up to his full lips? Rough? Prickly?

The thought of their tongues touching, lapping, tussling each other for dominance made the space between her legs tingle. In her head, she imagined him whispering in her ear, his breath tickling her neck. *Finley, do you want me to make love to you?*

"Finley? Finley?"

"*Yes, Cash.*" she said, in a moan "*I do.*"

"You do…what?" he asked.

Finley jolted when she realized she was no longer in her own head. "Umm, I…want you to keep encouraging me. Maybe you'll eventually convince me I can do this."

Cash stood. "Come with me," he said, guiding her out of her seat. "I know what will give you some clarity."

Did he have a bottle of Prosecco in his

office? Because right now, that was the only perspective she needed.

Inside the spacious kitchen, several people were hard at work kneading, mixing, frosting, and decorating desserts she was sure tasted as great as they looked. The aromas were intoxicating. Cinnamon, vanilla, citrus, and an array of other fragrant ingredients wafted around her.

"Ready to bake?" he asked.

Whipping her head toward him, she said, "Bake? I don't bake." Heck, she barely even cooked, despite actually being quite good at it. There were so many food delivery services available near her, she rarely had to turn on the stove. A hot meal was a mere phone call away.

"Wash your hands," he said, clearly ignoring her protest.

Well, it wasn't like she had anything better to do. Doing as he instructed, she joined him at a stainless-steel prep station. Cash stood directly in front of her. At over six feet, he towered over her five-seven frame. She drew in a lungful of his pleasant scent when he draped white apron strings around her neck. He smelled of fresh bread and…cardamom?

"Lift your arms," he said, wrapping the long strings around her torso and tying them in a front-facing bow. "You look nice in an apron."

When he punctuated the compliment with a sexy wink, Finley's stomach quivered. Demanding her body to cease and desist, she eyed the spread of ingredients on the metal table: flour, baking powder, sugar, salt, cinnamon, eggs, vegetable oil, milk and vanilla extract. "So, what are we making?" she asked. When Cash didn't respond, she glanced up to see him studying her. The way he regarded her warmed her from the inside out. "What?" she asked, a tiny smile curling her lips.

He shook his head. "Nothing." Turning his attention to the table, he continued, "We're making mini waffles first. They're what I'll be offering at the Chi-Flavor Afro-Caribbean Carnivale in Chicago. With my own tasty twist on them, of course. I want your opinion."

"I forgot you were leaving for Chicago next week. You and, um, Destini, right?"

Destini was Cash's lead decorator and accompanied him to most events he attended. As much time as the two spent together on a daily basis, Finley was surprised they hadn't hooked up. Well, at least as far as she knew, they hadn't. The thought rubbed her the wrong way. But she had to remember, Cash was not hers to claim.

Finley pretended to read the Madagascar vanilla extract bottle, hoping Cash hadn't noticed the hint of…something in her voice.

"Actually, no. I mean, yes, she was supposed to accompany me, but her father fell ill. Then Hunt was supposed to go, but he sprained his ankle. Romeo's wife is about to deliver at any second. Unfortunately, I can't spare anyone else. We have a ton of orders due next week."

Finley eyed him. "So, you're going alone?"

"Looks like it. That or cancel. I prefer to fulfill my obligation."

Before her brain had time enough to warn of the dangers of spending several days alone with Cash on a road trip to Chicago, she blurted, "I'll go."

CHAPTER 2

Cash did a double take of Finley, her eyes closed, head reclined back, the July breeze from the open window whipping through her hair, a look of contentment on her face. The midday sun gleaming off her skin gave her an angelic appearance. Had she always been so damn beautiful? Well, that had been a dumb question, because she had.

His eyes combed her jawline, imagining how her skin would taste as he peppered kisses against it. His perusal continued down the length of her neck, another place he would love to plant his lips. When his gaze landed on the swell of her ample breast, he stirred below the waist.

What in the hell had he been thinking to allow the woman he'd fantasized about for months to tag along with him to Chicago? It had been clear and present danger from the beginning, but like a fool, he'd ignored it. Something told him he'd pay dearly for his stupidity.

He could do this. He'd just view it like any other time they'd hung out together. This was no different. Though a lie, the affirmation was something he wanted desperately to believe. He pulled his eyes away from her before his undeniable attraction to her got him in trouble.

She's clearly waiting for you to make the first move, son, but no woman will wait forever.

His father's words had played on repeat in his head ever since he'd said them almost a week ago. *Dammit, old man. This is all your fault.* But had his father been right? Was Finley waiting on him? His desire was there, but was hers? Cash had never felt this type of all-consuming attraction for any other woman before. Not even Chandler.

The thought of his ex-fiancée made his jaw tightened with anger. He recalled the words she'd said to him the night she'd returned his engagement ring. *You're not the same man you used to be.* Of course he hadn't been. Life had changed him. But it hadn't been the mental change she'd been referring to; it had been the physical one. Even if she'd refused to admit it.

How had he ever fallen for a woman so shallow? The answer came swiftly. At one point, he'd been just as self-absorbed as Chandler. Thankfully, he was no longer that superficial jerk.

"What's wrong?"

The sound of Finley's voice pulled him from his thoughts only to realize she was staring at him. He shook his head. "Nothing. A little tired."

"Would you like for me to drive?"

"We're almost there," he said. Plus, she needed a commercial driver's license to operate the overweight food truck. But he appreciated the offer. She was always so considerate.

Finley pushed her brows together. "Almost there?" She glanced at her watch. We've only been on the road for like what, two hours?"

He nodded.

"So how are we almost there?" She narrowed her eyes in a playful manner. "What are you up to Cassius Jabar Warren?"

Her use of his full name reminded him of his late-mother. He'd lost her too, but unlike Jaicee's, his mother's death hadn't been his fault. Pushing the dreadful memories aside he forced a grin. "You'll see, Finley Rosette Cooper. Be patient."

"You of all people know patience is not one of my strong suits."

"I promise it'll be worth the wait."

"Ugh."

He shrugged as if to say, it is what it is. Finley stared at him, a tiny curl to her beautiful lips. Like a flick moving in slow motion, her eyes lowered to his mouth, but shot up at full frame speed as if she'd realized what was happening.

The elation present on her face moments ago vanished, replaced by a look of alarm. What had spooked her? the fact that he'd witnessed her action, or that she'd done it at all.

This time, it was his turn to ask the question. "What's wrong?"

"You're so tempting."

His head snapped back in surprise. "Excuse me?"

Finley's eyes doubled in size. "I mean testing. You're so testing."

"Hmm. I don't know. I think I like being tempting better."

"Just drive."

Cash could tell she was fighting to conceal a smile. He chuckled and refocused his attention straight ahead.

A couple of hours later, the mountains peaked in the distance. Finley sat forward in her seat and squinted as if confirming she was actually seeing what she thought she was seeing.

"It's mountains," she said, absently. "They're beautiful."

The declaration seemed to be more for her benefit than for his.

"You've never been to the mountains?" he asked.

She shook her head.

"Well, if you think this is beautiful, you'd love the Blue Ridge Parkway. To me it's far more beautiful in the Fall when the leaves have turned, but it's nice now, too."

"Can we go?"

"Not in the food truck. Vehicles with any advertising displayed on the body aren't allowed on the Parkway. I guess they don't want people distracted."

"Makes sense." Her face lit up again. "I'm happy I get the opportunity to see this." She swept a hand in front of her.

He wished they'd been in his pickup instead of this heap of metal so she could experience the awe of the BRP firsthand. However, she would get a great view of the Blue Ridge Mountains where they were headed.

When they arrived at the historic Omni Grove Park Inn, Finley's mouth fell open. And he could see why. The massive stone structure with the red clay roof was impressive. The lush landscape so green it looked freshly painted. He'd recalled her mentioning this place a time or two in regards to some kind of annual gingerbread house competition held here, and how she'd love to visit the century-old resort one day. While they weren't hosting any kind of competition during the three days they would be here, he figured the visit would still be just as meaningful.

"I hope you don't mind deviating from the course a little," he said.

Originally, he'd planned to make the almost thirteen-hour drive straight, but when Finley had volunteered to accompany him, he'd decided to turn it into an adventure for the both of them. Plus, it had been a long time since he'd visited the mountains. A place he used to love. There was something about the air up here.

Finley looked confused. "What are we doing here?"

"This is my way of saying thank you," he said.

Her dazzling eyes danced with excitement. "You're serious?"

"Yes. Let's go."

After giving the valet explicit instructions on handling Gemini—the name he'd given the custom food truck—they went inside to check in. The interior held its own level of exquisiteness with period furnishings that gave it a rustic feel. The front desk clerk rattled off several of the resort amenities—golf course, spa, indoor and outdoor pools, tennis courts, outdoor adventure center, restaurants, and bars—before directing them to the suite he'd reserved.

Cash had considered getting two separate rooms, but figured Finley would prefer their sharing a space. Ha! Who was he kidding? He was the one who preferred it. Until now, he hadn't considered how selfish he'd been.

"If you're more comfortable, I will get you your own room," he said as they rode the elevator up the adult-only Club Floor.

"I could never be uncomfortable around you," she said.

Her words touched him. "Good."

Entering their suite, Finley performed a full circle inspection. "Wow. This is…amazing."

Cash had to agree, and at eight hundred a night, he wouldn't have expected anything less than the fully-equipped kitchen, formal dining room, separate sitting area with a gas fireplace.

Finley moved to one of the wood-trimmed windows and peered out at the picturesque view of the Blue Ridge Mountains. "Just wow."

A moment later, she turned toward him with a look of concern on her face. "What's wrong?" he asked, closing the distance between them.

Tender eyes stared up at him. "You know you didn't need to do this, right? I overheard how much you're paying for this suite."

He slid his hands into his pockets and rocked back on his heels. "I think I have just enough in my piggy bank to cover it."

Thanks to the funds he'd received from the sell of his lucrative architectural firm, money would never be an issue.

Finley eyed him several more seconds before returning her gaze through the window. "Destini is going to hate she missed out on this."

Cash swore he heard a twinge of something present in Finley's voice at the mention of Destini. This hadn't been the first time he'd noted a variation in her tone when discussing his lead decorator. What was it? "No, she won't, because this particular excursion was planned just for you."

She tossed him a quick glance over her shoulder, then sent her gaze back through the window. "This sure is one grandiose thank you gesture for simply accompanying you to Chicago."

"This isn't just about Chicago, Fin. This is a thank you for everything you've done for me the past two years. I've had some rough days these past couple of years, but you were always right there, cheering me own. You deserve this and more. You'll never know how grateful I am to and for you."

Her head rotated toward him again, something tender in her eyes. "We're family."

The family label was like a gut punch from a heavyweight champion. Did it mean she viewed him as a brother? There certainly wasn't anything brotherly about his feelings toward her. But hey, maybe he had needed to hear this. Maybe now, knowing how she regarded him, would shake some sense into him.

For the first time since Cash could recall, his father had been wrong. Finley wasn't waiting on him.

*

Something had haunted Finley for the past hour, that flash of disappointment she'd seen on Cash's face when she'd referred to him as family. It had been quick, and had she blinked, she would have missed it. Anyone else probably wouldn't have noticed it, but she noticed everything when it came to him.

While family may be how her head viewed him, her heart certainly did not. But what was she supposed to say? Friends hadn't sounded prestigious enough, and soul mates would have sounded far too creepy. Family had been the only logical alternative, because there was no way she could have told him what he truly meant to her. That would have been unnecessarily awkward.

What had started as a beautiful friendship had blossomed into so much more for her, but she had to purge Cash from her system. Things were great between them, but history told her this type of harmony wouldn't last. It never had for her. She and Cash were too…perfect.

Finley recalled how several women had ogled him out in the lobby when they'd checked in earlier. What had swirled inside her had been undeniable jealousy. Had she rolled her eyes at the women any harder, they would have popped out of their sockets.

Something she hadn't given much thought to before, popped into her head. The fact that Cash wouldn't stay single forever. What happened when he started dating? Would she still have a place in his life? Would she want one? Could she put herself through the torture of watching him cozy up to another woman day in and day out?

Finley gnawed at the inside of her jaw as something more pressing filtered into her head. What if he proposed? Surely, no wife would want him in constant communication with his female friend—that was like family—but a female, nonetheless.

The thought of it all knotted her stomach. As far as she could tell, there was only one option. Once they returned from Chicago, she'd have to put some distance between them. Actually, a second option existed, telling Cash how she truly felt and hoping for the best.

No, she was too much of a coward to risk his rejection. Besides, if Cash was interested in her, wouldn't he have made a move by now?

Two light taps sounded at her bedroom door. Gathering her thoughts, she said, "Yes?"

"Are you ready? The car is here," Cash said from the opposite side of the door.

The mere hum of his voice caused a warm sensation to wash over her. How in the hell had she allowed this man to get into her system like this? Oh, she knew how. Like Cash, she'd had some rough days, too. Cash had been right there for her as well.

"Car?" Finley mouthed to herself. "Car?" she repeated, this time aloud. "Where are we going?"

"Patience," Cash said.

"Ugh. Do you not know me at all, man?"

"Probably better than you'd like for me to."

She wouldn't argue with that.

"Come on, woman. We're losing daylight."

When Finley opened the door, she needed to take a second or two to appreciate the man standing in front of her, wearing a navy-blue golf shirt, jeans, and dark brown casual boots. Not only did he look fantastic, he smelled spectacular as well. Like soap, cologne, and sweet temptation.

Cash had said to dress casual. Clearly, they'd both been on the same wavelength because she wore a blue shirt, too, hers being more of a royal hue, along with jeans and comfortable tennis shoes. They looked purposely coordinated.

Finley placed her hands on her hips. "I should refuse to leave this room until you tell me where we're going."

Cash unapologetically scanned her from head to toe. His dark eyes felt as if they were caressing her entire body. The tingling that started between her legs unnerved her a bit.

"Have you ever been hoisted into a man's arms and carried across the room?" he asked.

The air seized in her lungs. It was several seconds before she could respond due to the visual planted in her head of him hauling her across the room, to her bed, stripping off her clothes and making uninhibited love to her. "Um, no, I... No."

"Well, that's exactly what's going to happen if you don't come of your own free will. Something tells me it would look awfully peculiar moving through the hotel with you in my arms."

He had no idea how tempting the threat was.

"Well, in that case..." She ambled past him. "Let's go. I would hate for you to throw your back out carrying me."

"Trust me, I could handle it," he said, an air of confidence in his tone.

She tossed a glance over her shoulder, her eyes sliding over his broad shoulders and defined arms. No doubt he could. "What's in the backpack?"

"Essentials," was all he offered.

Finally making their way downstairs, they moved toward a shiny black SUV. The windows were tinted so dark it was impossible to see inside the vehicle. A middle-aged gentleman waited by the back passenger's side door and opened it as they drew nearer. She felt like a dignitary climbing inside the vehicle with its plush peanut butter colored seats.

Once settled in, they were off.

From the inside, Finley could see everything outside the window crystal clear. Asheville whipped by like a flag in the wind. She couldn't even begin to guess where they were headed because she wasn't familiar with the area. Wherever they were destined, she hoped it involved food.

"So, how many more *thank you* gestures do you have up your sleeve?" she asked, shifting toward Cash.

Cash stopped tapping on his cell phone. Before the screen went completely black, she saw an image of a Ferris wheel. Casually sliding the device into his pocket, he pointed to something outside her window. Glancing over her shoulder, she eyed a gray and blue sign that read: Entering Blue Ridge Parkway.

"I couldn't bring you all the way here and not have you experience the Parkway," he said.

Finley lowered the window, the comfortable seventy-five degrees kissing her skin. She couldn't recall ever regarding nature with such amazement. Clearly, God had taken extra care in crafting this beautiful oasis. Colorful pink and purple flowers bloomed amongst a vibrant background of green for as far as the eye could see.

After several miles, the SUV slowed and veered into an area designated for parking. Finley noted the sign that read Rough Ridge Overlook.

"Are you up for a little walking?" Cash asked.

"Yes. I'm dressed for comfort."

Outside the vehicle, Cash directed her onto a bridge with a small waterfall flowing underneath. The structure started their short, but strenuous uphill hike. She made a mental note to get back into the gym.

It was a good thing she wasn't afraid of heights, because Cash led the way out onto a massive boulder. They'd past several along the trek where people sat on the edges their legs dangling over the sides. She recalled thinking how insane they were. Not wanting to tempt gravity, she stayed a good distance from the ledge. "This view," she said.

"Amazing, right?"

"Breathtaking."

She took in the splendor. Her eyes swept the bluest sky she'd ever seen, admired clouds so fluffy they looked fake. The sounds of nature swirled around her. Singing birds, chirping crickets, rustling landscape. Closing her eyes, she inhaled deeply, the clean fresh air filling her lungs. Tilting her head back, she enjoyed the heat of the sun on her cheeks.

"Are you hungry?" Cash asked.

The sound of Cash's voice anchored her back to reality. Turning, she said, "Starv—"

The sight before her snatched the rest of her sentence. Cash had somehow arranged sandwiches, chips, fruit, and water right under her nose.

"Where did all of this come from?"

"I'm kind of resourceful," he said with a wink.

The backpack, she remembered. His

essentials. Finley eased down, the warm boulder heating her backside. Just when she thought the day couldn't get any better. She couldn't believe she was having lunch on a rock hundreds of feet off the ground. Had they been two people in love, the gesture would have been ultra romantic. But they weren't two people in love, just friends.

For the next couple of hours they chatted, laughed, and shared comfortable bouts of silence. Sitting here, staring out at mountains that spanned for miles, Finley couldn't think of any other place she'd rather be and any other person she'd rather be here with.

CHAPTER 3

Cash had assumed that after the adventurous time they'd had the day before, Finley would have wanted to spend today relaxing. Instead, she'd popped up at the crack of dawn, ordered him to get dressed, then directed him to a waiting SUV. It had felt like déjà vu, especially when she'd refused to tell him where they were headed.

"Patience," she'd said, using his own approach against him.

After a ten-minute drive, they arrived at a place called The Salt Space. Was it a restaurant? They'd already had breakfast, and at ten thirty in the morning, it was too early for lunch. When they entered, Cash realized it wasn't a restaurant at all, but some kind of spa. Alarm set in. Had Finley scheduled massages? God, he hoped not, because there was no way he would remove his shirt.

A friendly-looking, older woman with flowing jet-black hair welcomed them and introduced herself as the proprietor Margie. They were reserved for something called halotheraphy, which Margie explained in layman's terms as sitting in a dark room inhaling salty air.

"I love when couples experience halotheraphy together. To me it says you're truly invested in each other's wellbeing. It's refreshing to see. So many relationships lack that nowadays. We do have couple's massages inside the cave, if you're interested."

"Um, we're not actually a couple," Finley said. "Just, um, friends. That's all."

Margie's thick brows furrowed. "*Really?*"

"Friends that are like family," Cash offered, instantly regretting how sarcastic he'd sounded.

Finley eyed him strangely, her brows slightly furrowed.

Margie studied him, then Finley, then smiled. "I see. Well, I apologize for assuming. I must be losing my touch. I'm usually never wrong about these things." Margie swept her arm toward a corridor to their right. "Shall we?"

They both nodded.

Margie led them toward what she referred to as the Himalayan Salt Therapy Cave. The woman rattled off some of the wide-ranging benefits of such therapy: treatment for respiratory conditions such as asthma, bronchitis, allergies, as well as reduced inflammation in the lungs, an effective treatment to ease depression and anxiety. Cash wasn't sure he bought into the claims, but

Margie spoke with such conviction, it was hard to not at least consider their legitimacy.

The term cave fit the space appropriately. The dim light washed the room in a golden glow. The floors and walls were covered top to bottom in Himalayan salt—fifty tons, Margie informed. Soothing music played in the background. If Cash had to guess, the temperature in the room was about seventy degrees. Dry, but comfortable.

He breathed a sigh of relief when he learned they wouldn't need to disrobe. Taking their seats in zero gravity chairs, they were instructed to relax, release all stress and tension, and aim to achieve peace and balance for the next hour.

Obviously, he'd accomplished just that, because the next thing he knew, Finley was nudging him awake. Stretching, he said, "I think I dozed off a couple of minutes."

"A couple of minutes?" Finley laughed. "You slept the entire hour. Actually, two hours. When Margie came in to end our session, you were sleeping so peacefully I asked if the room was available longer."

He glanced at his watch. *Damn.* In his defense, he hadn't slept all that great the night before. His thoughts had been plagued with memories of their day together and how right it had felt being with Finley. Then he'd had a dream about her that was so hot he'd been forced to take a cold shower to rid himself of a painful erection.

"I'm sorry. I guess I didn't realize how tired I was." He had to admit, he felt fully energized now. Maybe there was something to halotheraphy after all.

The remainder of their day whizzed by like a whirlwind, touring on a big purple bus, lunch at a café where playing boardgames at the table was encouraged, watching street performers, and visiting several art galleries. By the time they returned to the hotel around seven that evening, he was exhausted. But instead of insisting they go directly to the suite, he suggested they enjoy a drink on the hotel terrace.

The view from the outdoor locale was almost as breathtaking as the one from Rough Ridge Outlook. However, sitting on a boulder hundreds of feet in the air gave Rough Ridge the advantage.

"You want to hear something strange?" Finley asked, taking a sip of her Chardonnay.

Being that he had a long drive ahead of him, Cash had opted for a local craft draft. "Sure?" he said.

"I haven't once stressed out about being unemployed since arriving here. And I really should be stressing out right now. But I feel so…unbothered by all of it. This mountain air is amazing."

"Do you remember what you told me when I first took over Jaicee's pastry shop?"

"These muffins do not taste anything like Jaicee's," she said.

Cash laughed. "That too, but I was referring to the part where you told me there's no need to stress, because you had my back." He eyed her. "Do you remember saying that?"

She nodded. "I do."

Cash shifted in his wicker chair and captured her hand into his. A warm sensation traveled up his arm. "Finley Rosette Cooper, there's no need to stress. I've got your back."

Finley stared at him long and hard, her beautiful face unreadable. For a moment, he thought she'd cry. He prayed she didn't. He could handle a lot of things, but a woman's tears wasn't one of them. Before the desire pulsing through him caused an avalanche, he released her hand. When he did, he swore a look of disappointment quickly flashed across her face.

"Do you remember the first time we met?" she asked.

Cash ignored the randomness of the question, but oh yes, he remembered. His sister's annual birthday party. Thinking back, Cash barked a laugh. "How could I forget? If memory serves me correct, you called me a pompous, inconsiderate jerk, whose ego was so swollen you were surprised my big head could fit through the door without damaging the frame."

Finley buried her face in her hands. Allowing her arms to fall, she said, "In my defense I did apologize. But you kind of deserved the insult."

"*Insults*, with an s," he corrected. "And how did I garner such a brutal characterization?"

"Are you kidding me? You walked around the party like you were the king mackerel swimming in a pond full of guppies."

He chuckled. "Yeah, I was kind of an asshole back then, huh?"

"Oh, you're being far too kind," she said.

"Damn, you're hard on a brother."

They laughed.

"Well, obviously, you did something right that night. You had every woman in the place vying for your attention."

Not every woman, he said to himself.

"Wasn't that the night you met Chandler."

Cash stiffened at the mention of his ex's name. He took a swig from his bottle and stared straight ahead. "Yeah, it was."

A reel of that night played in his head. Chandler had arrived with some of his sister's friends. The exotic-looking woman with the green eyes had caught his eye, along with half the other men in attendance. Watching her move in the skin-tight red dress that sparkled like a thousand tiny diamonds, he'd made a vow to have her in his bed that night. And he had.

Clearly, she'd been his punishment for being so damn cocky.

Cash drop-kicked the memory out of his head. "You were there with what's his name."

"Joseph," Finley said.

Yeah, that was his name. Despite not having known the man, Cash disliked the weasel. The entire night of the party, Cash had noticed him giving far more attention to other women than he had Finley. Once, Jaicee had vented to him about the serial cheater and bum—her words—and how he hadn't deserved Finley. He remembered wondering what Finley saw in the jerk that had kept her from leaving him.

What had finally given her the strength to walk away from him? Or had he left her? No, it had to be the former. Only a fool would sacrifice a woman like Finley. While he would have considered himself and Finley close, she'd never mentioned Joseph, and he'd never asked.

One day the man was there, then he was gone.

Finley looked to be lost in her own thoughts, so he didn't disturb her as she stared almost trancelike out toward the mountains. Her expression turned sad, like a person recalling a painful memory. What troubling thoughts were racing through her mind?

"I'm not sure I've ever seen a sunset more beautiful," she said. When she blinked, a tear rolled down her face. Swiping a hand across her cheek, she laughed. "I think this second glass of Chardonnay is taking its toll. I get emotional when I drink."

Cash wasn't convinced it was the alcohol, but he didn't attempt the pry the real reason from her. "Are you ready to go up?"

She nodded.

After a nice, hot shower, Cash checked in on Finley before he called it a night. She was curled up on the sofa, wearing an oversized night shirt and lime green fuzzy slipper socks. The scene made him chuckle because it was so Finley. Her face was buried in the novel she'd purchased on their trip downtown. A thriller by her favorite author. The book was as thick as a tractor tire. The crazy thing was, she was halfway through it.

Even in a generic nightshirt, hair pulled back into a ponytail and wearing reading glasses, she still took his breath away. His eyes did a slow crawl along her body, lingering several seconds on her soft brown thighs. *Friends*, he said to himself. *Just friends.*

"Is it any good?" he asked.

Finley yelped, tossing the book in the air. "Cassius Jabar Warren!"

He burst into laughter. "I'm sorry. I didn't mean to startle you."

Removing her readers, she placed them on the table. "You scared the heck out of me. I thought you were a serial killer coming to hack me into tiny pieces and feed me to his pet pig."

What in the hell kind of book was she reading? "Why do you read books that scare the heck out of you?"

Coming off the sofa, she closed the distance between them. "The book didn't scare me. *You* scared me," she said, pressing her index finger gently into his chest.

Finley smelled sweet, like citrus and vanilla. Having her this damn close was hazardous to his health. He willed his body not the react to the nearness. Despite that, his chest filled with heat, and his stomach knotted tight. "Well, if it makes you feel any better, I'll protect you from any and all serial killers determined to hack you into tiny pieces and feed you to their pig."

"Promise?"

Her voice was low, sultry and spellbound him like a siren's seductive song. "Promise."

A beat later, Finley pressed her soft lips to his. Stunned by the move, his body went rigid, but didn't stay that way for long. Despite knowing he was wide awake, the moment felt like a wonderful dream. Her warm mouth lingered against his for what felt like an eternity, but in actuality was probably no more than ten seconds.

Rearing back, she watched him. He couldn't decipher whether she was trying to engage his interest or waiting for him to make the next move. Lead by lust instead of logic, he crashed his mouth down on hers.

The kiss was more than he'd ever imagined. And boy had he imagined kissing her, along with a laundry list of other naughty things he'd fantasized doing to her. He circled his arms in a tight hold around her body. Their tongues danced in deliciously intoxicating harmony. Finley's moans took him to another level of excitement. But when Finley lifted the hem of his shirt, he catapulted from his desire-driven state and pulled away.

Fine lines creased Finley's forehead as confusion played on her face.

"I can't," he said, so dazed he wasn't sure if he'd actually said the words aloud or in his head. But when Finley brushed past him in almost a sprint, he had the answer.

Finley's bedroom door slammed. He closed his eyes and ran a hand over his head. *Dammit.* Escaping to his own room, he fell back onto the mattress and eyed the ceiling. Removing his phone from the nightstand, he sent Finley a text. A cowardly approach, but he couldn't bare seeing the same disappointment in her eyes he'd witnessed moments ago.

I'm sorry.

He waited.

Several seconds later, his phone chimed, indicating an incoming message. A simple thumbs up icon filled his screen. Tossing the phone aside, he shook his head. *Great. She's pissed at me.*

Kissing Finley, he'd felt such a connection to her. And not necessarily on a sexual level, though that link was pretty damn strong too. So, why in the hell had be pulled away? Pushing from the bed, he moved into the bathroom, removed his shirt and eyed his burn scars in the mirror.

Fear. It was the only explanation he had.

He ran his hand along the darkened skin that started just under his shoulder blade to his waist, where he'd suffered full thickness burns—or third-degree burns as many called it.

While the skin grafts and use of compression therapy had minimized scarring, he would always have a visual reminder of that horrific night.

It honestly terrified him that Finley would give him the same look of repulsion Chandler had when she looked at his disfigurement. Yes, he knew Finley was nothing like his ex, and he desperately wanted to believe the scars wouldn't faze her, but could she see past them?

Just as he exited the bathroom, his cell phone chimed. Retrieving it, he saw that another message from Finley had arrived.

I'm sorry, too. And embarrassed. It seems I keep making mistake after stupid mistake. She punctuated the sentence with a shrugging emoji. **Nothing has changed, I hope. Let's just forget tonight ever happened.**

*

Finley wasn't sure she could have been more mortified if she'd accidentally walked into a room filled with monks wearing nothing but her smile. But even then, she could have brushed her blunder off as an accident. Not now. When she'd kissed Cash hours ago, it hadn't been a mishap. It had been very much intentional.

The sting of his rejection still lingered. How in the hell could she look at him for the next several days and pretend everything was okay? That everything was the same? She couldn't. Climbing out of bed, she moved toward her suitcase. Cash would probably hate her for abandoning him, but she had to leave.

A soft knock at the bedroom door froze her in her tracks. Of course she knew who it was, but why was he here? Had his rejection not been enough? Did he come to further humiliate her? Actually, she couldn't fault Cash. She'd done this to herself by kissing him. But he'd kissed her back. In a way that held no regret. So why had he pulled away?

Crossing the room, she took a deep breath, exhaled, then pulled the door open. The instant her eyes locked with his, the kiss replayed in her head. Her knees wobbled a little.

"Can you tell me with a straight face it was a stupid mistake?" he asked.

It surprised her that Cash was even at her door asking this, because he'd been the one to pull away. "It must have been. You rejected me, remember?"

"I didn't—" He stopped abruptly, his Adam's apple bobbing from a hard swallow. His tone was level again when he said, "I didn't reject you, Finley."

She folded her arms across her chest in a defiant manner. "Really? Okay. Well, what would you call someone pushing you away and saying they can't?"

Cash appeared to be mulling over the question in his head, but she had no doubt he'd come up with the same answer she had. *Rejection.*

"I have my reasons," he finally said, in a tone so low she barely heard him.

Pushing the gambit, she said, "Is that all I get? A blanket statement?"

Cash's jaw flexed several times as if he were trying his best to keep whatever words wanting to be freed from escaping. What could be so devastating that it pained him this much to reveal?

"I gave you an out, Cash. To forget the kiss ever happened. Take it." She took a step back into her room. "Good night, Cash," she said, before closing the bedroom door.

"I lied to you. To everyone," he said.

When she reopened the door, he continued.

"I didn't break off my engagement to Chandler, she broke it off with me."

Finley's head jerked back in surprise. Not because it had happened—she never thought he and Chandler were a good fit anyway—but because he'd felt the need to lie about it. He'd told her that he and Chandler had grown apart, wanted different things out of life, and had mutually parted. The explanation had seemed plausible.

"I don't get it, Cash. Why would you lie about that?"

"I was ashamed," he said.

Ashamed? Had he done something to end their engagement. Had he cheated on her? "Why did she call off the engagement?"

They stood in strained silence for several seconds.

"Because of this," Cash finally said, removing his shirt.

Finley's eyes widened slightly at the sight of his chiseled chest, dusted with fine black hairs. Her fingertips yearned to explore him. A warm sensation washed over her and settled between her legs, awakening a need. His ripped midsection reminded her of a rugged mountain range she'd love to climb. As much enjoyment she got out of ogling him, she didn't get how his chest had caused their breakup. "I don't understand," she said, forcing her gaze up to meet his.

Cash turned. Obviously, this was what he'd wanted her to see. When she moved closer and ran her fingertips over the textured surface of his skin, he flinched. She snatched her hand away. "I'm sorry. Did I hurt you?"

"No," Cash said, his head hung low.

She realized that she'd probably been the first person who'd ever touched him here. Her fingers returned and she moved along the area from his shoulder to his waist, as if she were reading Braille. When she placed a delicate kiss to his skin, he swayed, as if the action had been too much for him to handle. She placed several more kisses to his imperfect skin. A puff of air escaped from Cash, as if he'd been socked in the stomach.

"You thought your battle wounds would turn me off?" When he didn't respond, Finley snaked in front of him. The look on his face was a mix of hurt, pain, sadness, and a hundred more emotions. "Cash?"

"They sent my fiancée packing," he said.

"You should know me better than that."

"I thought I knew Chandler."

"Chandler and I are two *totally* different people, Cash. I'm not sure what she saw when she looked at you, but I see a hero. A man who risked his own life to pull a mother and her two kids from a burning vehicle."

Finley would never forget the night of his accident, because it had also been the night her best friend—his sister—had died in an automobile accident on her way to the hospital. Regret and guilt still gnawed at her every time she thought about that night.

"I'm nobody's hero, Finley. Trust me."

"You are to me. And I sure as hell know you are to that mother and her two kids whose lives you saved. But I don't just see a hero when I look at you, Cash. I see a man who refused to allow his sister's dream to die with her, so he stepped out of his to build hers. I see a man who has always put family before all else. I see a man who would drive a food truck *all the way* to Illinois just to raise money for charity. I see *you*, Cassius Jabar Warren, and I've been too afraid to say this before now, but I kinda dig him on a massive level. And by the way you kissed me, Cash, I think you kind of dig me, too. And for the record, your wounds aren't enough to keep me away from you."

Cash cradled her face between his hands. He stared at her for several intense seconds before kissing her gently, cautiously. She wrapped her arms around him, never once bothered by the tickle of his scars against her forearm. As weird as it sounded, the sensation aroused her. Breaking their mouths apart, she said, "Kiss me like you really mean it."

Cash fully accepted the challenge. Gentle and cautious became urgent and determined.

The way he ravished her mouth ignited every inch of her body. Her taut nipples ached to be touched. The space between her legs throbbed. She yearned for a release.

Greedy for everything Cash offered, she met his demand, kissing him with every ounce of longing flowing through her. To make sure he understood exactly what she wanted, she inched a hand between them and cupped him.

Cash's erection seemed to grow even more solid in her hand. The thought she'd done this to him with just a kiss stroked her ego a bit. Okay, a lot, because she couldn't remember the last time a man responded to her in this way.

When she stroked him gently, a groan rumbled deep in his chest. Placing his hands on her ass, he squeezed hard, causing her to release her own pleasure-filled sounds. The second he broke their kiss, all Finley could think was please, not again. His labored breathing mimicked hers, like they'd both run a marathon and were worn out from the excursion.

"I'll give it to you anyway you want it tonight, Finley, all night, if that's what you require."

The thought of having him inside her all night was more than a turn on than she could ever imagined.

Cash went on. "But…"

Oh, God. No *but*.

"…I want the first time our bodies connect in this way to be nice and slow. Does that work for you?"

Cash's lust-laden eyes bore a hole right through her, his hungry stare caressing a part so deep, so delicate inside her, she nearly came right then and there. "All I want is you. It doesn't matter how you give it to me, so long as I get all of you."

Her words must have triggered something inside him, because with one swift motion, he had her in his arms. Once inside the bedroom, he placed her back on her feet. Displaying little urgency, he lifted the nightshirt over her head. Folding it in half, he moved across the room and delicately draped it over the arm of the chair by the window.

Instead of returning to her, he watched her from across the room, his gaze raking over every inch of her nakedness. The moonlight filtering into the room outlined his gorgeous body—wide shoulders, impressive chest, long, sturdy legs—and also washed the room in a romantic golden glow.

While Finley knew no one could see them from their high-floor room location unless they stood on the mountains in the distant using a telescope equipped with night vision, the idea of making love to Cash with the windows wide open for the world to see, made her tingle even more. When she took a step toward him, he flashed a palm.

"Stay there," he said.

Compliant and confused, she stilled.

His daunting eyes drank her in from head to toe. "You're beautiful."

Her cheeks warmed. She felt a little too vulnerable at the moment. "Thank you."

"This is probably too much, too soon, but I've imagined you naked, standing in front of me just like this so many times, that I feel as if I've explored you a thousand times before."

He'd imagine her naked? Countless times? "Is it as delightful in real life as in your fantasies?"

"Better. Way better."

Wordplay had never done anything for her, but Cash's words were doing everything to her. "Would you like to touch it?"

"Oh, I have. I've cupped your breasts. Ran the tips of my fingers along your stomach. Glided my hands over every luscious curve." His gaze settled between her legs. "Caressed the most intimate part of you."

The air grew heavy in her lungs, and she could barely breathe through the thick veil of want and need smothering her.

Cash took a step forward. "In my head, I know every single inch of your body. In my head, I know exactly what it'll take to please you. In my head. In reality, I don't know any of these things. So, I need your help." He took another measured step toward her.

"M-my help?" It was the only sentence she could form.

He nodded, moving even closer. "You're going to remember this night, Finley Rosette Cooper. That I can promise you."

Clearly, some of that ego still lingered.

"But I don't want you to simply remember it. I want you to feel it anytime this moment filters through your head."

Oh, she had a good suspicion she would.

Toe to toe, Finley could feel the heat wafting off Cash in sheets. When he rested his hands on either side of her waist, the jolt caused her to draw in a sharp breath. He gave her a wicked smile as if he knew exactly the effect he was having on her.

"If I'm not touching you how you like, teasing you how you want, tasting you how you need, tell me." He dipped his head pecking her softly on the lips. Rearing back, he said, "Teach me." He peppered delicate kisses along her chin to her ear. Kissing the spot below her lobe, he whispered, "Will you do that for me?"

"Yes."

CHAPTER 4

Cash scooped Finley into his arms again. This time, carrying her to the bed where he placed her down gently onto her back. The mere sight of her spread out in front of him did crazy things to his body. It had been so long since he'd been this damned aroused. He couldn't wait to slide inside her, make love until they both reached their breaking points.

Taking his time with Finley was not only appealing, it was necessary. It had been a while since he'd been intimate, close to two years to be exact. As worked up as she had him, if he didn't pace himself, it would be over before it ever really began.

"I need to go to my room a second." And by go, he meant run like hell. When a look of disappointment spread across her face, he smiled a little. Clearly, she wanted him just as much as he wanted her. It felt great to be wanted. "I'll be right back."

Inside his bedroom, Cash retrieved the box of condoms from his suitcase he'd packed just in case. *Wishful thinking.* Not wanting to waste another second, he removed his pants and underwear before returning to Finley.

"What took you…" Finley's words dried up and her eyes settled on his erection. "…so long?" she said absently.

"I'm here now," he said, tossing several foil wrappers on the nightstand.

Finley came up on her knees, wrapped her arms around his neck and kissed him hard. After several seconds, she broke away and kissed a line down his torso. When she took him in her mouth, a primal growl rumbled in his chest.

"*Shit*," he said. His fingers tangled through her hair. Closing his eyes, he allowed his head to fall backwards. The sensation of her taking him in and out of her warm, wet mouth was almost too much to handle. "Finley…" The muscles in his stomach tightened with each oral stroke, warning him that if he allowed this to continue, he would shatter.

In one tactical maneuver, he had Finley on her back, her arms pinned above her head. Positioned between her legs, he could feel the radiating warmth of her core against his erection. Like a heat-guided missile, his dick twitched toward her opening. Two things stopped him from entering her right then, he'd wanted to take his time with her, and he wasn't wearing protection.

"Do you have any idea how damn good that

felt?" he asked.

"So, why'd you stop me? I was just warming up."

If that was just her *warming up*, he'd definitely made the right call by stopping her. He trailed his fingers down her arm, along her collarbone, and across her nipple. Goosebumps rose on her skin. He teased the hard pebble with the pad of his thumb right before sucking it into his mouth. She moaned.

After paying equal homage to the opposite breast, he licked, nipped, and kissed his way to her most sensitive spot. Her delicious scent intoxicated him, made him dizzy with desire. The tip of his tongue circled her engorged pearl, then suckled her gently. Finley writhed and cried out his name.

"Do you like that?" he asked, kissing her inner thigh.

Finley released a sound that mimicked a sob. "Yes. Oh, God, yes. I love it."

Cash smiled at her response. Hugging her hips to keep her in place, he feasted on her like he'd never feasted on a woman before. His intense hunger for her grew by the second. He raged with a need to make her come. And she did, screaming with an intensity he felt in his chest.

Finley's back arch, body quaked and

trembled, but he continued to work his tongue with the same determination as before.

"Cassius!" Her hands clamped against the back of his head, pinning it in place. "Oh, God, Cassius. I'm coming…again."

Moments later, she cried out. This release apparently capsized her, because she went limp. Her body still quivered as he kissed his way back to her mouth. A thin layer of sweat glistened on her skin, leaving the taste of salt to linger on his lips.

Finley's eyes fluttered open. "That was amazing," she said, her voice hoarse and low. "I want you. I've never wanted a man the way I want you."

Unable to hold back a second longer, he retrieved a condom and ripped the foil open with his teeth. His shaky hands threatened to betray him, but cooperated long enough for him to unroll the rubber down his length. In one swift, delightful thrust, he was inside her. They moaned in unison.

Cash claimed her mouth in a heady kiss, moving in and out of her with slow, deep strokes. He glided in and out of her with ease, her wetness providing the perfect lubrication. If she felt this good with a barrier between them, what would she feel like without one? And could he handle that?

Unlatching his mouth from her, he said, "I can feel you, Finley. All over. What the hell are you doing to me, woman?"

"Making you mine," she said. "All mine."

"I've been yours for a long time," he whispered in her ear.

Finley whimpered, her nails digging into his damp flesh. The sting, more pleasure than pain, caused him to lose his composure. His strokes increased in speed and intensity. When Finley's muscles tightened around him, he tried his best to hold on a little while longer. But when she came undone—pulsing around him—so did he. In all of his years of having sex, he'd never been so gripped by pleasure that he'd called a woman's name until now. Finley's name bounced off the walls.

Collapsing onto the bed, he pulled Finley into his arms. Neither uttered a single word. There was no need. They'd both said all they needed to say, through words and actions. He was hers and she was his.

*

The following morning when Finley stirred from sleep, she instantly felt the effects of Cash's absence from the bed. Mostly because his strong, protective arms were no longer wrapped around her.

She squinted against the blinding morning light pouring through the window. Closing her eyes, she snuggled up with one of the feather pillows. *What a night*, she thought, a wide smile curling her lips. The ache between her legs reminded her that it hadn't only been the night. Sleep, make love, sleep a little less, make a little more love. It had been their routine into the wee hours of the morning.

Finley eyed the numbers on the clock. *8:30.* Collectively, she'd only gotten a good three, maybe four, hours of sleep. But, man, had the deprivation been totally worth it. She hated they had to leave Asheville today but knew Chicago would be just as memorable. As long as it wasn't all work and no play.

The sound of running water drew her attention toward the closed bathroom door. Untangling from the covers, her stiff muscles growled, evoking a memory of all the many ways her body had twisted and turned for Cash. The man was one hell of a thorough lover who'd known exactly how and where to touch her, like they'd been exploring each other's bodies for years.

Dragging her naked body across the floor, she crept inside the bathroom. The warmth of the room felt great against her chilly skin. Cash stood inside the oversized shower, both palms braced against the stone wall, eyes closed, head dipped down, water cascading over his magnificent body. The scene awakened her delicate parts.

She took several moments to appreciate every powerful inch of him: wide shoulders, ripped arms, strong back, muscular thighs and calves, rock-hard ass. The space between her thighs ignited with a scorching need. After their satisfying night together, Cash inside her again should have been the last thing on her mind. But it was the only thing on her mind.

Tapping the glass with the nail of her index finger caused Cash to flinch. Obviously, she'd startled him. His head escaped the flow of water and his eyes opened and smiled when he saw her.

"Mind if I join you?"

A roguish grin lit his face as he pushed the door open and welcomed her inside. He scanned her from head to toe, a look of appreciation on his face. It filled her with unexplainable confidence. She pressed her wet body against his. "Do you know how beautiful I feel when you look at me that way?" The same admiration she'd witnessed in them the night before when he'd stood across the room and watched her.

"You are beautiful." He pecked her gently on the lips. "Sexy." He kissed her jaw. "And an absolute turn on."

Cash placed her hand on his solid erection, and a jolt of awareness shot through her.

"See what you do to me."

She bit at the corner of her lip. "Did you not get enough of me last night?"

"I'm not sure there's a such a thing as enough of you. My body responds to you in a way it has never responded to a woman before."

Cash's words filled her with a fullness she hadn't felt in a long while. "I think we should do something about this," she said, tightening her hand around his shaft and stroking him slowly.

He drew in a long, deep breath, grabbed a handful of her hair and kissed her hard. She walked him backwards until his back rested against the wall. Freeing her mouth, she lowered to her knees. With the tip of her tongue, she teased the head of his engorged penis. Circling, flicking, licking, sucking. The sounds he emitted were primal and music to her ears.

When she took him all the way into her mouth, his knees wobbled. Twining his fingers into her wet locks, moving his hands with the same cadence as her head.

"It feels…so…good. So damn good," he said, his head relaxing back.

The declaration made her even more determined to please him, finish what she'd started the night before when he'd stopped her. She didn't allow him to stop her this time until he careened over the edge, falling into a wormhole of pure ecstasy.

CHAPTER 5

Finley had to give Cash his road-trip planning props. Instead of their trip to Chicago feeling like a never-ending journey, it had felt more like an adventure. After leaving Asheville that morning, they'd ventured to Charleston, West Virginia. She'd heard so many negative things about the state that she'd been a little apprehensive about being there.

Her fears had been unfounded. Everyone they encountered had seemed genuinely authentic in their greetings and treatment. Cash fielded question after question about the food truck. She understood people's interest. The chocolate-colored mobile kitchen was state of the art. Stainless steel, generators, fryers, grill, refrigerator, freezer, ovens, and a sink. Honestly, she wasn't sure how it all fit together, but it did, and allowed for comfortable maneuvering inside.

They'd had lunch at a southern cooking restaurant Cash claimed he'd seen featured on the Food Network channel. Plaques on the wall confirmed it. She'd eaten her weight in ribs, pulled pork, sweet potato casserole, collard greens, baked beans, and smack-yo'-

momma mac and cheese. Anyone watching her probably thought she was eating for two.

All of that goodness had put her into a food coma, and she'd slept the entire three-hour drive to Dayton, Ohio. After an overnight stay in the Buckeye State, they'd hit the road again. Spending several hours in Indianapolis, Indiana, they finally arrived in Chicago Thursday afternoon.

After checking into the hotel, they decided to explore The Windy City a bit. The ride-share car dropped them at Navy Pier. The delicious aromas wafting from Giordano's—a Chicago-style pizza restaurant—greeted them the second they entered. Forgoing eating for now, they strolled the massive space. Finley made a note to purchase some cheese popcorn from Garrett before they left.

Cash purchased a VIP ticket to the Centennial Wheel, but when Finley saw the gondola had a glass bottom, she grew anxious about boarding. Cash kissed the back of her head and told her not to worry because he wouldn't let anything happen to her. It was enough to steady her quaking nerves. Settling into the plush leather seat, she said a little prayer to cover them both—just in case.

The iconic Ferris Wheel soared nearly two-hundred-feet into the air, providing a breathtaking three hundred sixty-degree view of the Chicago skyline and Lake Michigan. The view through the floor wasn't bad either. A monitor told the history of the Navy Pier and the wheel, but Finley paid little attention to it.

"Are you okay?"

She nodded. "Perfect."

"Yes, you are," he said, kissing the back of her hand.

No one spoke for a long while. Finley could tell Cash was deep in his thoughts because he absently smoothed the pad of this thumb back and forth over the back of her hand. Sliding a glance in his direction, his solemn expression suggested he was a hundred miles away. What was racing through his head?

"Do you have any regrets?" she said, drawing Cash's attention.

"Regrets?" His brows furrowed. "About what?"

"Us stepping over that friendship line."

"No." He watched her a moment. "Do you?"

His tone sounded a little grim, like he all but expected her to say yes.

"The only thing I regret is it not happening sooner," she said.

Cash's head jerked in obvious surprise. "How much sooner?"

"The night we met."

"*Wait, wait, wait.* You do recall putting me all the way in my place the first time we met, right? And a few times after that, if I'm remembering correctly."

"The only time you seemed to want to engage with me was when we were at odds, so I manufactured odds."

"So, you're telling me you've had a thing for me all these years?" he asked.

"No, not all of these years. Once you started getting serious with Chandler, I realized my window of opportunity had slammed shut, so I moved on."

His facial expression soured. "With that Joseph character."

"Yes," she said.

What she didn't confess to was that the only reason she'd gotten serious with Joseph was to get her mind off of him. What a big mistake that had been. In her attempt to avoid heartache, she careened right into it with Joseph. But it had been her own fault. With Joseph, she'd seen the signs, but like most women, had chosen to ignore them. It had cost her. Her dignity. Her pride. Her best friend.

Eyeing their joined hands, Cash said, "When you stopped coming around, I missed you." Meeting her gaze, he said, "A lot."

"I was avoiding you. It's what I needed to do."

"I get that."

A beat of silence passed between them.

"Did Jaicee know that you had this huge, relentless obsession with me?"

When he smiled triumphantly, Finley bumped him playfully. "Don't flatter yourself. But yes, she did. Or at least I suspected she did, because she always made it a point to tell me when you were coming over to her place. I always made it a point to be there. But she never called me out." Maybe if she had, things would have been different.

"It makes sense now," Cash said more to himself than to Finley.

"What makes sense?"

He chuckled and shook his head. "Why she didn't want me to be with Chandler. Jaicee used to say she wasn't sure Chandler was the right one for me, that I needed someone who would challenge me. I think she was trying to tell me I needed you."

*

Cash wished Jaicee was here right now. He would tell her she had been right; he did need a woman who challenged him. And now that he had her, he would never let her go. If anyone would have told him a month ago he would be here with the woman he fantasized about so much that she felt like a part of him, he would have called them insane. He would have made the claim, *we're just friends* as he often did with his father and uncle. They'd seen right through that cloak of deception.

Something expecting swirled in Finley's eyes. Was she wanting him to confess that he did need her? He did. In a way he'd never needed—or wanted to need—another person before. Could he tell her that she'd come to mean so much to him over the past two years that he couldn't for one second imagine life without her? Should he really shock the hell out of her and bare his entire soul and tell her he loved her, and not in a close- friend-like-family type of way either. He loved Finley with an earnest intensity that could topple a mountain. And it scared the shit out of him, because it left him too damn vulnerable, too damn exposed.

Love had been his tormentor once, and he'd sworn to never fall victim to its cruelty again. Yet, here he was, taking this risk. In his defense, Finley had made herself so easy to love. Even as friends, she'd shown him a type of compassion and dedication he'd never known in any intimate relationship he'd ever been in. As daunting as loving her seemed, he wasn't sure he had any other choice. She'd somehow embedded herself so deep inside of him that he felt her with every breath he took.

Could he make such a sincere declaration so soon? No, he told himself. The time would come. At that moment, he wouldn't hesitate for one moment pouring out his soul to Finley.

He searched her beautiful face. Fire blazed through him. He'd never experienced anything like this from simply staring at a woman. Never felt an all-consuming passion, need, desire to just be near her. Not even Chandler, the person he'd been prepared to spend his life with. Finley was his paradise, refuge, his strength and his weakness. With all the power she had over him, would she break his heart?

The Ferris Wheel slowed to a stop, jarring him from the dark depths of his thoughts. Refocusing on Finley, he gave a half smile. "Jaicee always loved being right."

An easy smile blossomed on Finley's face.

Several hours later, they strolled arm in arm along the pier. A gentle breeze blew off Lake Michigan, a welcome relief against the warm July evening. The fading sun painted the horizon in an ambient blue, purple and orange.

"This feels like a first date," Finley said. "Minus all the awkwardness, of course."

"In that case, we should take some time to get to know each other better."

Finley looked at him with happy, quizzical eyes. "Are you serious?"

"That's what people do on first dates, right?"

"But we already know each other."

"We can always learn more. Humor me," he said, directing her to one of the many wood and steel benches scattered throughout the space.

Seated, Finley shifted toward him. "Okay, Mr. Warren, what would you like to know?"

Without skipping a beat, he said, "Everything."

Cash knew trivial things about her. But what he wanted was to learn were the significant details, things she'd shied away from sharing with anyone else, even Jaicee. He wanted to know what made her tick, her fears—and not just the surface ones she'd already shared—spiders, scary movies, clowns. He wanted to know it all, because he wanted to learn her, fully understand who she was outside of the Finley he already knew so well.

"I wasn't expecting that," she said. "Most men don't take the time to get to know their woman. At least that's been my unfortunate experience."

"I'm a curious man."

They both became geysers.

She shared.

He shared.

They shared.

Finley told him about her childhood and the loneliness that came along with being an only child. Shared with him that she had never known her father. Talked about her mother—a nurse who'd worked her ass off to make sure Finley never went without. Mentioned her grandparents, whom she spent most summers in South Carolina with.

In return, he'd told her how Jaicee used to always fight his battles when they were kids, because he was too timid to stand up for himself—a not-so-glowing revelation. He confessed how at twelve he'd once stolen a bag of M&Ms from the corner store and how his father had made him work in that same store every day after school for three months to make amends.

They talked for hours about everything. The Good. The Bad. The Ugly. But all of it was okay, even the unpleasant and draining parts, because it was like they recharged one another, gave each other the strength and courage to keep sharing.

"Tell me about your mother," Finley said.

"Jaicee used to talk about her all the time. She sounded like a wonderful woman."

The mention of Erthal Warren made Cash's heart swell. "She was the first woman I ever loved. My mother was to me what Disney World is to a bright-eyed child. Larger than life. Her smile could push light into the darkest heart. Her laugh was infectious." For just a millisecond, he could hear the sweet sound ring in his ears.

"Now I know where you get it from," Finley said.

"Get what?"

"The ability to captivate." She leaned in and kissed him on the cheek. "Tell me more."

"All anyone in the neighborhood had to do was hint at being in need and my mom was preparing meals, taking up collections, starting a prayer chain. I asked her once why she did those things."

"What did she say?"

"That sometimes God just puts things on your heart."

A wave of emotion forced him to pause a bit. He didn't understand the true value of all of the moments he'd shared with his mother until this very moment. Leaning forward, he rested his elbows on his knees and took a moment to breathe. Being the nurturer she was, Finley slid close and smoothed her hand up and down his back. Her touch soothed the storm inside of him. "How do you do that?" he asked.

Finley's brow furrowed. "Do what?"

"Make everything better."

She rested her head against his back and wrapped her arms around him. "I'm sorry," she whispered.

"For what?"

"For dredging up painful memories."

"They're not painful. Just overwhelming." He maneuvered Finley into his arms, kissing her at the temple. "Our mom is where Jaicee developed her love for baking. Those two would bake a cake for anything. Regardless of the occasion. They once baked a honey cake for World Honey Bee Day."

Finley reared back to eye him. "World Honey Bee Day? I didn't know that was even a thing."

"It's in August, in case you were wondering," Cash said.

"I love honey," Finley said.

Cash considered a few ways he'd like to use honey. None of them involved food. All of them involved Finley.

"Jaicee is the reason I love orange-cranberry muffins."

"How so?" Cash asked.

"I was having a day from hell when I saw this new pastry shop and decided to stop in and feed my anguish. I'd ordered chocolate chip cookies. Obviously, Jaicee took one look at me and knew I needed something more. After I was seated, she brought over an orange-cranberry muffin and eased down. She said I looked like I could use a friend."

"Yeah, that sounds just like Jaicee."

"Needless to say, the shop became my favorite place and Jaicee became my best friend. All thanks to an orange-cranberry muffin."

"It's our mother's recipe," he said.

"I didn't know that," Finley said.

"She used to bake tons of those cupcakes every Christmas and pass them out as gifts. Adding it to the menu was Jaicee's way of honoring her."

"I miss her so much."

Cash held Finley tighter. "So do I. She loved you like a sister."

Finley's voice cracked when she said, "I loved her the same. Thank you for keeping her memory alive, Cash. You could have easily sold the shop and carried on with your life, but instead, you chose to honor her memory by stepping out of your dream and into hers. I commend you for making such a sacrifice."

"Thank you for saying that."

Outlandish as the move may have been, it had felt…necessary. Jaicee had entrusted him with something that had meant the world to her, and he had been determined to make her proud. Especially when he'd been the reason she was no longer there to celebrate her accomplishment.

Giving up everything he'd known, what he'd been educated to do—was great at doing—to run a pastry shop hadn't been easy. Countless times he'd questioned his decision—and his sanity—but something had always kept him pushing forward. He chose to believe it was the relentless spirit of Jaicee watching over him and guiding his steps. He'd be damned if he would fail her again.

A baking and pastry course at the local community college had given him the tools he'd needed. He'd used them to build something amazing. For him, the peace and serenity he'd found in pastry arts was priceless. It was by far one of the best moves he'd ever made.

To lighten the mood, he said, "Are you ready for tomorrow? It shouldn't be too crazy, I don't think."

"Yes, I am. I've never been to an event like

this before. Or worked a food truck. I'm excited."

Silence descended on them for a spell, but that was okay. Cash stared out at Lake Michigan, hypnotized by the water. While droves of people peppered the pier and chatter swirled around them, it was like he and Finley were the only two people there. It was the best feeling in the world.

CHAPTER 6

At the crack of dawn the following morning, Finley and Cash arrived at Huntington Bank Pavilion at Northerly Island—a ninety-one-acre man-made peninsula along Lake Michigan's waterfront and where the festivities for the Chi-Flavor Afro-Caribbean Carnivale would kickoff. Games, rides, and vendors occupied the expansive space. The entire scene excited Finley, taking her back to her childhood, and how excited she got when the carnival came to town. Hopefully, she'd get an opportunity to unleash her inner kid.

Her job today was to take orders, collect money, and continue to look gorgeous—as Cash had advised—while his was to focus on the mini cinnamon waffles being offered. With the sample she'd tasted at the shop a week ago—and had helped tweak—she knew they would be a hit. The petite treats were being offered with an array of toppings: fruit butters, Belgian chocolate fudge sauce—her favorite—berry compote, and rum-infused whipped cream to name a few. It was a creatively delicious spin on the classic. To complete the dish, every waffle would be dusted in fine powdered sugar, because *anything sugar coated is always better*, Cash had said. She would have to agree.

That morning, they'd seen a steady flow of visitors, but by lunchtime the line wrapped around the truck.

"What the heck is going on?" Cash asked when Finley delivered another stack of orders.

Finley had a suspicion about what was fueling this rush. "I may have initiated a teeny, tiny social media campaign before we left North Carolina." She pinched her thumb and index fingers together. "Teeny, tiny."

Cash stopped what he was doing to eye her. "Teeny, tiny?" He barked a laugh. "Babe, the line is a mile long. If we keep going like this, we're going to run out of supplies."

She smiled a bit at him calling her babe. Shrugging, she said, "Sorry, not sorry."

"Come here," Cash said. When she was close enough, he leaned in and kissed her on the lips. "You're always looking out for me. Thank you."

"You're welcome," she said, stealing a quick peck and heading back to the order window.

"Hey," Cash called out.

She turned. "Yes?"

"This is proof you're going to rock the hell out of your new company. Now get back to work, woman." He punctuated his words with a wink.

Around three that afternoon, Cash decided to shut down the truck for an hour. It excited Finley that she would get the opportunity to visit some of the carnival-type games. Plus, she was starving. The smell of grilled onions and peppers had teased her all day. While she'd stolen a waffle or two, she needed meat. Her lips curled into an easy smile. She would have loved Cash's meat, but since that wasn't an option, an Italian sausage dog would have to do.

Her arm wrapped around Cash's waist and his draped around her shoulders. They moved through the maze of games and food concessions.

"What do you have the taste for?" Cash asked.

Finley glanced up at him. "What I have a taste for is not on the menu."

Mischief gleamed in Cash's eyes and he dipped his head low to kiss her. Pulling away, he said, "I'll satisfy that particular hunger tonight, and I won't stop until you are full."

The mere image of rolling around in the bed with Cash, tangled in his arms, sent heat rushing through her body. She'd never been with a lover who satisfied her so completely, known spots she liked touched, and ones she had no idea she liked explored. Cash's kisses, licks, nips, touch was all she craved now and the idea of having to wait didn't please her one bit, but she would be patient because he was well worth the wait.

An Italian sausage with onions and peppers, an ear of corn drenched in butter, and a jumbo lemonade later, Finley was stuffed. However, it didn't stop her from taking a bite out of Cash's grilled turkey leg. The succulent meat was delicious, but wasn't better than her meat-filled hoagie. When he offered one of his French fries, smothered with cheese and topped with jalapeños, she'd passed.

"It's game time," Cash said.

Finley and Cash managed to fit in several games before they needed to return to the truck. Balloon darts, ring toss, and whack-a-mole to name a few. Cash had been determined to win her a large stuffed animal during a target shoot game. Poor thing wound up spending far more than what the pink elephant was worth. But he didn't seem to mind.

"What's your fascination with elephants anyway?" Cash asked.

"They're interesting animals."

"How so?"

"Well, for starters, they're highly intelligent.

They only need four hours of sleep. Despite their size, they're gentle creatures."

"An elephant gentle?" Cash said. "I've seen some videos showing these *gentle creatures* being mighty aggressive. *Especially* the females. *Especially,*" he repeated.

Finley bumped him playfully. "That's because they were probably being taunted or they're calves were near. Like humans, female elephants are protective over their children. If it were a bull—an adult male elephant—it was probably musth."

"Musth?"

"It's when a bull has heightened aggression because of a surge in testosterone level." When Cash looked confused, she said, "They're horny and want to screw their brains out."

He grinned. "*Ahhhhhh.* Well, I guess that makes me a bull." He lowered his voice and moved closer to her ear. "Because I'm horny and want to screw *your* brains out. But let's keep that between us."

Finley tossed her head back in laughter. "Your secret is safe with me."

*

When sight of his food truck came into view, Cash stopped in his tracks. "What the hell?"

Several women—and by several, he meant at least thirty—waited.

"Don't be mad," Finley said.

With the way she'd started—urging him to keep his cool—Cash knew he probably wouldn't like what followed. "What did you do?"

"When you were getting your turkey leg, I may have sent out a message that you'd be taking pics around this time, along with one of the sexiest images of you I had in my phone."

Cash tensed a little. Finley had snapped several pictures of him over the past four days. Most of them with his shirt off. Before he could ask, she pulled out her phone to show him which one. It was the one she'd taken when he stood at the bathroom entrance, his arms above his head, holding the frame of the door in unbuttoned jeans and shirtless. His scars, while not prominent—were still visible.

Instantly, anger swelled inside him. "You had no right to do that, Finley," he said, his words sharp. "You should have asked me if I wanted my image plastered all over the internet. I would have said no."

Finley jerked in apparent shock, forcing him to regret how terse his words had been. Still, he held to his stance. If he'd wanted the world to see him exposed like this, it should have been his call to make. When the look of joy on her face faded to sadness, he regretted even more snapping at her.

Shit.

With a much calmer voice, he said, "I'm sorry. It's just that—"

"I get it," Finley said, cutting his words off mid thought.

He wasn't sure she did.

Finley continued, "You're right. I shouldn't have violated your privacy like this. I'll get rid of them."

While her face didn't show any signs of bother, her eyes did. They no longer danced with the brilliance they had earlier. He hated he'd been the one to snuff the light from them. She started to move away, but he caught her by the hand, pulling her back to him, wrapping one arm around her, hoping to lessen the sting of his words.

"It's the scars, right?" Finley said.

Well, maybe she did get it after all. He nodded.

"Cash, you are not your scars. They don't make or break you as a man. They don't value or devalue you. When I look at you, I don't see your scars."

"What do you see?" Because he couldn't

look at himself in the mirror without seeing them.

Finley rested a hand on his chest. "Your heart."

He could literally feel the sincerity in her words.

"For me, those scars add to your ruggedness. They also remind me of how selfless and courageous you are. Quit wearing them like a scarlet letter and start wearing them as your badge of honor."

Cash swore he fell in love with Finley just a little more. He was truly a blessed man to have a woman who spoke life into him.

"There is so much more to you than your scars, Cassius Jabar Warren. I have no problem with them. Obviously, they don't either," she said, tilting her head toward the growing crowd of women.

Pulling his gaze back to Finley, he rested his hands on either side of her neck and stared deep into her eyes. "I…" He paused a moment thinking about his next words carefully. "…am a lucky man." *And apparently a coward,* he thought, because while the statement was true, they hadn't been the words he'd been poised to say. "Let's do this."

Finley ran the quote, unquote photo shoot like a pro, getting each woman's permission to use the pictures in promotional material. Each had eagerly agreed, excited as if they'd just been cast in a film that would inevitably become a blockbuster. Finley also asked everyone to share to their social media platforms and urge their followers to pay them a visit.

To watch Finley was mesmerizing. Not only because her body drove him wildly insane with lust, but the way she dealt with people. It awed him how good she was at connecting with strangers. Several times, he'd overheard Finley being asked if they were a couple. Several times he'd smiled at her response. *Yes, we are.* Unfortunately, their status had obviously not mattered to some because he'd tossed at least seven phone numbers he'd been slipped. He was a many of things, but a cheater had never been one of them.

When Finley ended the event, sounds of disappointment emitted from the individuals who hadn't gotten an opportunity to have their picture snapped. What in the heck had Finley posted to have these women regarding him as if he were some kind of celebrity? He made a mental note to read her post.

For the remainder of the day, a steady flow of patrons kept them busy. By the time they called it a night, he and Finley were both exhausted. After a quick, but thorough, cleanup job, they returned to the hotel.

Walking toward the hotel, Cash stopped.

"What's wrong," Finley asked, hoisting See-Saw—the name she'd given her pink elephant—up on her hip as if he were a child.

"I'm just curious," he said.

"About?"

He shifted toward her. "Whether or not you've ever been kissed under a star-filled sky on a warm July night." When Finley tilted her head heavenward, he fought the urge to drag his down the length of her neck, nip her tender skin with his teeth, leave his love mark prominent enough for any other man to see, to know that she was taken.

"No."

Finley's low voice guided him back to reality. "Good," he said, right before lowering his mouth to hers. His tongue eagerly invaded the warm space, exploring it like a man in search of something. She moaned, making him even more eager to claim every single inch of her. Dropping See-Saw to the ground, she wrapped her arms around him. He could have kissed her all night, and probably would have, had someone not yelled, "Get a room."

They laughed against each other's mouths.

Cash pulled away and stared at her. "Maybe we should get a room."

"Sounds like a good idea to me."

Entering their room, Cash collapsed onto the sofa. He'd planned to rip Finley's clothes off the second they entered, but he wasn't sure he had the energy to lift the shirt over her head.

Finley eased down on top of him. "Oh my God. I'm not sure I've ever been this tired," she said, nestling her head in the crook of his neck. "*Mmm*. You smell like cinnamon."

"Is it turning you on?"

"So much. If you let me take about an hour nap, I'll have the energy to show you how much."

They shared a hearty laugh.

Of course he didn't admit to his need for a nap, too. "I guess I can wait that long. I'm thinking we open a little later in the morning. That way we can catch the parade." He was sure most folks would be at Soldier Field for the parade kickoff anyway.

Finley's head popped up. That spark he'd grown to love so much danced in her eyes.

"That would be awesome."

He brushed a stray hair away from her face. "Thank you for today."

"You don't have to thank me. But I do owe you an apology. I should have never posted your shirtless picture without your permission. I just saw the beauty in it. I didn't consider your feelings."

Initially, he'd been upset the image had been posted for the whole world to see, but Finley's words had made him feel whole, and for the first time in a long time, his scars hadn't mattered. "I owe you an apology, too," he said.

Her brows bunched. "For what?"

"Snapping at you. That'll never happen again. Do you forgive me?"

She nodded. "Yes."

Finley kissed him gently, then pulled away. Staring into her eyes he felt so much peace it startled him. "What if I told you I—"

"Yow!" Finley said, jolting.

"What's wrong?"

Finley laughed. "My phone vibrated." She laughed again, fishing the device from her back pocket. "I have a voicemail. Do you mind?"

Cash shook his head. He looked on as Finley's facial expression went from jovial to serious to quizzical. The second she disconnected, he said, "Is everything okay?"

"It was Madison. She wants to meet with me. This Wednesday if I'm available."

"Are you going to meet with her?"

Finley shrugged a shoulder. "I don't know. I'm curious to know what she wants."

"You know what she wants. For you to return to her agency. She knows letting you leave was a huge mistake. If she asks you to return, what are you going to say?"

Finley looked as if she were mulling over the question before finally saying, "I'm not sure."

"Well, if you want my unsolicited opinion, I think you have everything you need to successfully run your own agency. Knowledge. Experience. Determination. Just look at the amazing job you just did. I'll support whatever decision you make, but don't walk away from your dream because you're afraid. I'm your biggest cheerleader. Go, Finley," he said, shaking imaginary pom-poms.

Finley giggled like a schoolgirl. Sobering, she said, "Speaking of the event, we should see if folks are posting pics from today." She tapped the screen several times. "Wow."

Dammit, this woman wouldn't be satisfied until she gave him a heart attack. "What?"

Finley showed him the screen. "Wow."

He was amazed by all the images, shares, tags, and new likes to his page. Finley read some of the comments aloud, feigning jealousy at some, laughing at others. The audacity of some of the posters astounded him. Clearly, they couldn't care less about the fact that things put on the internet were there forever.

Several posters raved about having taken a picture with him, others about the mini waffles, one person hash-tagging their review of them with the words *sugar coated love*. It was kind of catchy.

"Some women have no shame," Finley said, tossing the device aside and nestling against him again. "Can you believe some of those comments? Just scandalous."

Cash fastened his arms around her, kissing the top of her head. "Are you jealous?"

"Maybe a little."

"Look at it this way, they only get to fantasize about me, you get the real thing."

"That makes me a really lucky woman." Her brows knotted. "What were you going to tell me? Before my phone nearly sent me into cardiac arrest."

He was about to lay it all out on the line until something occurred to him. What if she didn't feel the same? That would make for one awkward as hell drive back to North Carolina. Deciding to hold his confession until they were back home, he said, "I just wanted to tell you your hour's up."

CHAPTER 7

Saturday morning, Finley and Cash stood amongst the mass of people present at Soldier Field to watch the parade. Women of all shapes and sizes donned vibrant costumes in a myriad of colors. Red, green, purple, pink, yellow, blue. The list could go on and on. They really were putting the color in life. Finley gained a renewed love for feathers, seeing some of the headpieces. Many were absolutely exquisite. Large, full, and showy.

But it wasn't just the woman claiming showstopper status. The men were just as impressive in their attire, wearing costumes with oversized, warrior-type headdress in bold, energetic colors. Most were shirtless, displaying muscular physiques that did nothing for her.

A plus-sized woman in a bright yellow, orange, and gold two-piece costume, revealing more than it concealed, caught Finley's eye. She loved how the dancing diva radiated with pure confidence. *Slay, queen, slay*, she wanted to scream. She doubted she'd have been heard over the thunderous music anyway.

Several bands performed, each one as good or better than the last. The Caribbean tunes made it impossible to stay still, and Finley moved to the rhythm of it. Cash rested his hands on her hips and grooved along with her. It was as erotic as one could get in public. Grinding her ass against his crotch, she felt his erection grow. The thought of his arousal heightened her own. Too bad it would be hours before he could satisfy her needs.

"Do you know how bad I want you right now?" Cash said into her ear, his voice slightly above a whisper.

"Oh, I think I have a good idea," she called back, reaching behind her to cup his shaft through his jeans. The feel of him—long, thick, hard—sent her pulse racing. Cash groaned then pushed her hand away. She laughed.

"You'll pay for that tonight," he said.

"Is that a promise?"

He kissed the tender spot below her earlobe. "Absolutely."

After the parade, Finley and Cash were back to slinging waffles. Today's sales rivaled yesterdays within the first three hours. Several patrons mentioned learning about the tasty treats through friends who'd visited the day before or had seen a post on social media.

Finley had impressed herself with how well the *secret* campaign had gone. Well, all except for the picture thing. Initially, she'd been upset at first, but the more she thought about it, Cash had had the right to be peeved at her.

That afternoon a journalist visited Cash's food truck after getting wind of his delicious cinnamon waffles. Finley enjoyed watching him talk about something he clearly loved. Creating culinary goodness. It always tickled her a little when she considered the fact that the flour slinging, cinnamon sprinkling, chocolate drizzling man used to be an architect before giving it up to become a pastry chef—a job he was excellent at. Could he fail at anything?

A professional photographer slash filmmaker snapped several candids of them at work along with video. They'd signed a release waiver, giving him permission to use the footage. Finley felt like a star in her very own romantic comedy flick.

Several local artists took to the outdoor stage and played into the evening, delivering phenomenal performances. DJs battled it out for bragging rights, driving the massive crowd insane with their talent. A spoken-word poet brought Finley to tears with her unique way of delivering her life story. With so much positive energy flowing on Northerly Island, the atmosphere was electric. She loved every second of it.

The second they stepped inside their hotel room that night, Cash had her back against the closed door, kissing her like it had been a privilege he'd been denied for far too long. It took only a millisecond for her body to react to him. Her nipples beaded inside her bra and the space between her legs pulsed. Heat rushed through her like lava on a path of destruction. When he deepened the kiss, a moan of pure satisfaction escaped. God, she loved the way he kissed her.

Unrestrained.

Determined.

Raw.

Breaking their mouths apart, she said, "I want you, Cash. Right now." Judging by the hungry look in his eyes, he wanted her, too.

Moving in silence, Cash lifted her shirt over her head and tossed it aside. Instead of removing her bra, he knelt and sucked one of her hardened nipples through the black, lacy fabric. She whimpered from the sensation that cut through her like a scalpel. Why was he torturing her like this?

Returning to a full stand, he removed his shirt, then unbutton his pants. When she tried to push them off his hips, he blocked her, then flashed a devious grin that sent her libido into overdrive. "Do I have to beg?" she said in a whimper.

Still, nothing. The silent treatment he was

giving her was both arousing and frustrating. She needed him to tell her what to do to get what she wanted. Her entire body throbbed with desperate need.

The next several moments were all a blur, Cash removing her bra, pants, lowering to his knees. When his warm tongue teased her through her panties, awareness shot up like a rocket, along with her heart rate. Her heart pounded against her ribcage, breathing grew labored, skin clammy. If she hadn't known better, she would have sworn she was having a heart attack.

As Cash glided his tongue along the silky fabric, he snaked his finger into the damp material and inside her. She cried out, her limbs trembling with anticipation of the release she desperately needed. His finger-stroked her with unhurried momentum.

In and out.

In and out.

In and out.

It drove her wild.

For the first time since he'd started along this path of ecstasy, Cash spoke, his voice husky, heavy. "You're so damn wet, so damn ready for me, huh?"

"Yes, Cash, yes."

A beat later, he ripped the thin material from

her body. The action almost made her come right then.

"I hope they weren't your favorite pair," he said.

Fuck those panties, she wanted to scream. She also wanted to tell him to do the same to her.

Cash spread her with his fingers and placed a delicate kiss to her clit. When he peppered kisses up her naked body, panic set in. *No, no, no.* What was he doing? He couldn't get her all wet, willing, and wanting, and leave her like that. In one swift swoop, she was in his arms. Obviously, he'd read the alarm on her face.

"Don't worry, I would never leave you unsatisfied."

*

Inside the bedroom, Cash lowered Finley onto the mattress, spread her legs wide and reclaimed his place between them. He feasted on her like her juices were the nutrients he needed to survive. Her moan, movement, taste—oh, her sweet taste—drove him delirious. And in the blink of an eye, he lost complete control.

His tongue twirled, flicked, lapped, licked. The more she squirmed, called his name, the more determined he became. When his tongue had claimed every single drop of her essence, he focused on her clit, sucking it between his lips over and over and over again.

She wailed, her body writhing underneath him. Placing her hands on the back of his head, she ground her sex against his mouth. Clearly, she wanted more. And he provided it, given her engorged sex more suction. The move did her in.

Finley cried out, back arched off the mattress and clamped his head between her thighs. Still, he didn't let up. Out of sheer greed, he continued savoring her until her body went limp. Then and only then did he free her from his hold.

Standing at the edge of the bed, he watched her chest heave up and down, her body quiver. It filled him with satisfaction.

Her eyes fluttered open. "That was amazing," she said. "Now I want you inside me."

Cash removed the rest of his clothes. Finley's hungry eyes took in every naked inch of him. When her gaze lowered to his swollen dick, she licked her lips.

"I want to taste you."

He shook his head. "No. I couldn't take it. Not right now. Not when I already want you so bad I'm about to bust."

"In that case, you better come and get me."

It was a challenge he couldn't refuse. Retrieving a condom, he rolled it down his length. Instead of joining Finley in the bed, he pulled her to the edge. Pushing her legs together, he lifted them in the air, then slid into her. With her legs resting on one shoulder, he moved in and out of her with long, hard strokes. In this position, she was so tight, felt so damn good, he wasn't sure how long he would last.

Finley seemed to be enjoying it just as much as he was. His name rolled off her sweet tongue again and again.

"Cash…"

"I'm here, baby. Right here."

He moved faster, harder, driving in and out of Finley as if he were trying to set a world record for endurance. The sound of flesh smacking flesh reverberated through the room, mixed with their cries. The room started to spin, but Cash was determined to maintain his momentum as long as he could. The sensation of an impending orgasm tingled in his loins, suggesting the time was near. And when he couldn't hold back one second more, he shattered into a thousand pieces.

Collapsing down beside her, Cash pulled Finley's quivering body into his arms. "Oh my

God, that was amazing," he said, his chest rapidly rising and falling.

With her voice just as heavy, Finley said, "Yes, it was. I think I've worked up an appetite."

"Me, too. Let's order room service."

Roughly an hour later, their food arrived. Pretzel bites with several varieties of dipping sauces, mozzarella sticks with a sweet basil marinade sauce, shredded chicken nachos, cheese smothered fries, roasted red pepper hummus and a buttery lobster roll.

"I'd never tried a lobster roll until I met Jaicee," Finley said.

"They were her favorite," Cash said. "Along with mozzarella sticks," he added.

As they enjoyed their meal, Cash and Finley laughed as they shared their fondest memories of Jaicee. It made Cash feel good to memorialize his sister this way. She'd touched both their lives deeply. When Finley's expression went from joy to sadness, he'd realized it had become too overwhelming for her to remember. He understood. The conversation was starting to take its toll on him as well.

"We can talk about something else," he said, caressing her arm.

Finley studied the mozzarella stick in her

hand. "Jaicee called me that night," she said. "The night she died," she added for unnecessary clarification. Her eyes met his. "I sent her call to voicemail."

Cash stiffened. Why had she intentionally sent Jaicee to voicemail? Had they had an argument or something?

Finley continued, "When I finally listened to the message…" Her words dried up a moment. "She was hysterical. All I could make out was something about an accident, your name, and her saying to please call her back as soon as possible." She blinked back tears. "God, I wish I had taken her call."

"Why didn't you?" Cash asked, suddenly losing his appetite.

Finley's eyes moved away. Why couldn't she look at him? When she did, the look on her face told him he would not like what she had to say.

CHAPTER 8

On Wednesday afternoon, Finley arrived at the VanBeran building. She took a deep breath before exiting her vehicle and heading to meet with Madison. At the moment, she still hadn't made up her mind about whether or not she would accept her old job back, if indeed that was why Madison wanted to meet with her. But she couldn't think of any other reason why the woman would want to see her.

Recalling Cash's words in Chicago made her smile. *I'll support whatever decision you make, but don't walk away from your dream because you're afraid.* He had no idea how much his words had meant to her. How in the hell had she gotten so lucky? She wished Jaicee was here to actually see her happy for a change. God knows her best friend had seen her miserable plenty with Joseph.

Finley wished she was back in Chicago. Better yet, Asheville. Crazy as it sounded, she was still exhausted from the trip back from Chicago. The event had ended that Sunday and they'd said goodbye to Illinois bright and early Monday morning. Unlike their trip up, they'd driven straight back to North Carolina, only stopping for bathroom breaks and food.

Obviously, Cash was still exhausted, too, because he hadn't quite been himself the past couple of days. Uncharacteristically quiet and a little distant. Finley didn't want to think the worse—that he'd had a change of heart about them—but something was up. She could feel it in her gut. And if that wasn't enough, she could feel it when they made love.

Was she losing him? The thought made her heart ache. No, she was being ridiculous. She and Cash were fine. Pushing the negative thinking aside, she chalked his behavior up to simply being overwhelmed and busy after having been gone from the shop for a week.

Using visitor protocol, Finley sign in at the security desk, received her visitor badge and made her way to the top floor. The security measure seemed like overkill for an ad agency, but Madison leased space to several other tenants. Having the added security measure appealed to the other occupants, as well as allowed her to charge just a little more. That was Madison. If she couldn't make a profit, it wasn't worth her time.

Waiting inside Madison's office, Finley noticed things she never had before. Probably because when she visited this space, it was usually under tumultuous circumstances. The color of the drapes, patterns on the chair fabric, or exquisite artwork had been the last things on her mind.

As expected, Madison kept her waiting. The same way she did clients she deemed unworthy of her time, Finley noted. She scoffed. Well, her time was just as important as Madison's. Just as she'd decided to leave, Madison entered.

"Finley, darling, I'm so sorry to keep you waiting. I had an urgent call I needed to take."

The well-put-together woman sashayed across the room in expensive-looking emerald green and gold heels and an equally pricey-looking button-down green shirt and deep blue pencil skirt. One thing was certain, no one could ever call the fashion police on the woman.

Madison eased into her chair and flashed a remarkable smile. "Thank you so much for agreeing to meet with me today."

In her head, Finley gagged over Madison's faux kindness, but kept her face unreadable. At least she hoped it was unreadable.

"I'm sure you're wondering why I've asked you here."

"Yes, I am a bit curious," Finley said, playing the older woman's game.

"Well, dear…" She stood and moved to the window, looking out. Returning her focus to

Finley, she continued, "I'm not too arrogant to admit when I've made a mistake. Finley, dear, I've made a mistake by allowing you to leave." She cupped her hands together. "There, I said it."

Finley nearly fell over in her chair. Madison VanBeran apologizing? The world had to have shifted a little on its axis. "I see," Finley said.

"I would like you to return," Madison said. Nearing her desk, she lifted a black and gold folder and passed it to Finley. "I think you will find this offer extremely generous."

Finley read the documents inside. A promotion to an executive position with her own team, four additional weeks of vacation time, a company car. Finley fought her reaction to the impressive salary increase. Almost fifteen thousand more than she'd been making as a manager.

In her head, Finley quickly filtered through the pros and cons of accepting Madison's offer.

Pro: I wouldn't have to go through the grueling process of starting a business.

Con: I would still have to deal with Madison.

Pro: I would have a guaranteed income.

Con: More pressure would inevitably be placed on me.

Pro: I would have my own team to lessen the

workload.

"So, what do you think?" Madison asked.

Finley parted her lips to accept Madison's offer, but heard Cash's voice in her head. *I'll support whatever decision you make, but don't walk away from your dream because you're afraid.* "Yes, this is an extremely generous offer."

A confident gleam showed on Madison's face.

"But I'm going to have to pass," Finley said. "I've decided to start my own agency." The huge decision she'd just made should have filled Finley with at least an ounce of regret. It didn't.

Madison's rigid posture, tight jaw, piercing stare told Finley the woman was doing everything she could to restrain from flying into a rage. In the past, Finley would have been shaking in her clearance rack heels at the woman's demeanor. Not now.

Finley stood. "Have a great day, Madison." Then walked away.

"You can't do this without me," Madison said.

At the door, she turned and faced the seething woman. "I can and I will."

Deep down, Finley knew she'd made the perfect move. She couldn't wait to thank Cash for giving her the strength and courage to do so. And because she couldn't fight it another second, she also planned to reveal that she loved him.

*

Later that Wednesday evening, Cash stood alone in the Pleasure Pastries kitchen chopping walnuts. He only ever processed them by hand when something lingered on his mind. Finley. Or better yet, what Finley had tried to tell him back in Chicago.

When she'd confessed to intentionally allowing Jaicee's call to roll into voicemail the night of Jaicee's accident, he'd felt some kind of way. But when she'd hinted at her ignoring the call had had something to do with her trifling ex, animosity flowed like a raging river through him.

With tear-filled eyes, she tried to give him the specifics, but he'd shut her down by pulling her into his arms and urging her to just rest. He hadn't wanted to hear anymore. In the tense moments that followed, he'd found himself blaming Finley for Jaicee's death. Of course not to her face. But he'd cast all the weight from his own shoulders onto hers.

Cash remembered all the questions that had scorched through his brain. What if Jaicee had been calling to ask Finley to drive her to the hospital, because she was too distraught to drive herself? Things would have been different. A jolt of anger sparked through him and he slammed his hand down on a walnut shell, cracking it wide open with the blow. Seething, he ignored the pain that radiated at the heel of his hand.

It wasn't two seconds later when his father burst through the door leading into the kitchen. Cash had forgotten the man had even been there, wiping down tables and sweeping the floor. The stressed expression on his father's face revealed his concern.

"Sorry, Pop," he said. "I didn't mean to alarm you."

His father moved closer, a look of concern on his face. "What's going on with you, son? You've been a little distant with everybody since you returned from Chicago. Did something happen?"

Cash had always been able to talk to his father about anything, so he filled him in on what Finley had told him that night. Confessed his feelings toward the situation. He purged it all, holding nothing back. It felt good to finally get it off his chest. But oddly, the more he talked, the more he realized how foolish he'd been to blame her. Finley missing the call hadn't caused Jaicee's death. He'd clearly needed someone else to blame, besides himself.

Before he could reveal any of this aloud, there was a ruckus out front. When Cash exited the kitchen to investigate, Finley stood there, her face wet with tears. He froze, his heart sinking to his feet.

What looked like what used to be a cake was strewn at her feet, as if it had fallen from her hands and exploded once it met the floor. "Finley?"

"You blame me for Jaicee's death?"

Her words were low, measured, shaky and laced with hurt. Tears glistened in her puffy eyes and she seemed to barely be able to look at him.

When he moved toward her, she flashed a palm, her delicate hand trembling. He stopped as if on cue. "Finley, let me explain."

"I felt you pulling away," she said, swiping her hand across her cheek. "But I thought—" Her words caught. "I thought you no longer wanted to be with me." She half sobbed, half laughed. "I was so scared of losing you, because I—"

She stopped, her words stalling again, but Cash knew what she'd wanted to say. She loved him. He loved her, too.

Finley shrugged. "I guess it no longer matters."

The cryptic comment scared Cash. What had she meant by that? What no longer mattered?

Finley's gaze fell to the mess at her feet. "It's early, but I baked you a honey cake. World Honey Bee Day," she added as if to remind him. "I..." Her red-rimmed eyes rose to meet his. "I need space." With that, she backed away, turn, and left.

CHAPTER 9

For the past week, every time someone walked in, Cash's eyes darted toward the door. And every time for the past week, he'd been disappointed. Finley hadn't visited the shop since she'd overheard him talking to his father.

He could barely breathe without her. She'd asked for space; he'd given it to her. But how much more time did she need? Her absence felt like a void in his life and a black hole in his heart. He missed her. Damn, did he miss her. Obviously, she didn't hold the same sentiment.

"Look at him. Over there looking like a lovesick puppy."

Cash paid no attention to his uncle. Honestly, he didn't care what he looked like. All he cared about was getting Finley back.

"Why don't you just call her, son?" his father asked as if it were just that simple.

Cash tossed the white rag he'd been using to wipe the same spot for the past hour, rounded the counter and joined his father and uncle at their booth. "She needs space."

Yes, he wanted to rush over to her place and use all the air in his lungs to beg her forgiveness, but he also wanted to honor her wishes. He'd already screwed up enough. Just to let her know he was thinking about her, he'd sent her a text message a couple of days ago. He was still waiting for a reply.

A part of him feared that when he saw her, she would drop a bomb on him. That they were over. The hurt he'd seen in her eyes made that a definite possibility. He didn't want to lose her, but he also couldn't make her stay some place she didn't want to be.

"Uh-oh," Uncle Rudolph said.

"Uh-oh, what?" Cash said.

"Don't pay him no never mind," his father said. "Every relationship goes through a rough patch. She may feel gone, but you haven't lost her."

Cash ran a hand over his head. "It sure feels like I have. I've never gone this long without talking to her."

"Oh, looka there, looka there," Uncle Rudolph said, eyeing a group of mature women who'd just entered. "Gentlemen, if you would excuse me. I think I see my next ex-wife." He scooted from the booth and clapped Cash on the shoulder. "I can put in a good word for you, nephew. On second thought... Those platinum cougars would devour a young pup like you."

When Uncle Rudolph smooth-walked off,

his father laughed. "He won't be happy 'til he's around here somewhere using his social security check to pay child support for a newborn."

The thought of his seventy-something uncle fathering a child made Cash cringe.

"Do you love Finley, son?"

Cash studied his father a minute. He could lie and say no, but knew the man would see right through him. What would have been the purpose anyway? "In a way I didn't even know could exist."

"Why?"

Cash pushed his brows together. "Why?"

"Yes, why? You can't claim to love a woman and not be able to look her in the eyes and tell her why."

Cash glanced away, studying his twiddling thumbs. "She makes me feel whole," he said. "Chandler broke me a little, Pop. I was convinced every woman would view me the way she had. Like damaged goods." He looked at his father again. "Not Finley. When she saw my scars…" He recalled how her gentle fingers moved over him, and how he nearly buckled when she'd kissed his wounds. "For the first time in a long time, it felt as if they didn't matter."

Cash effortlessly listed all the reasons why

he loved Finley. The more he talked about her, the more determined he was not to lose her.

"Son, you know how your mother and I lasted fifty-two years?"

"How?"

"Because we never gave up on each other. Sure, it was difficult at times. In those times, it would have been easier to throw in the towel, call it quits, move on to the next one. But your mother was worth all my energy. So I loved her hard. We loved each other hard. And that relentless love rewarded me with a lifetime of happiness, two beautiful children and memories that will never die."

Cash's chest tightened when his father massaged his eyes. He could count on his fingers the number of times he'd seen the man cry. All of those times had revolved around either his mother or Jaicee. He rested his hand on his father's forearm. "You okay, Pop?"

Eldridge nodded, then cleared his throat. "Are you happier with or without Finley?"

That was a no-brainer. "With her. I want to be with her. Unfortunately, I'm not sure what I want matters."

"Well, there's only one way to find out."

*

Finley never imagined being happy about all the work she faced to make her new company—The Mountain View Agency—a reality, but she was. Staying busy kept her mind off of Cash. She didn't want to think about him, because doing so only reminded her of how much he'd hurt her. How could he for one second blame her for Jaicee's death? How?

Unshed tears stung her eyes and she blinked rapidly to keep them from falling. It didn't work. They flowed freely down her cheek. Smearing them away, she decided to call it a night. It wasn't like she could focus anyway.

Just before heading to the bedroom, the doorbell rang. Moving to the door, she checked the peephole. When Cash's face filled the hole, she inhaled a sharp breath. What was he doing here? She wiped the wetness from her face. *Okay, pull yourself together.* A blink later, she opened the door, but only because he deserved to hear it from her face to face that they were over. She'd avoided this conversation, but obviously, the universe felt it was time she stopped running.

The second she opened the door, the scent of his cologne reeled her in. Something familiar swirled in her stomach and she reprimanded her body for responding to him. The dark gray polo shirt he wore highlighted his muscular arms. For a brief second, she missed them wrapped around her. While he was still as handsome as ever, he looked exhausted. "What are you doing here?" she asked, forgoing a greeting.

Cash slid his hands into his pockets. Several seconds passed before he said, "Um, hey. H-how are you?"

Ignoring his question, she repeated hers, "What are you doing here?"

"I love—"

She held up her hand and backed away. "Don't you dare say that to me."

Her words fell on deaf ears. Cash crossed the threshold and slowly moved toward her. "Finley Rosette Cooper, I love you."

She shook her head. "No, you don't."

He moved closer. "I love you."

And closer.

"I love you."

Anger swelled inside her and she lashed out. "Why do men always think saying those words will make everything all right. Why do they use them as a bandage to cover wounds that they've inflicted?" Her tone softened and tears spilled from her eyes again. "Why can't a man ever say those words and truly mean them?"

When she released a sob, Cash wrapped his arms around her and held tight. For just a moment, she allowed herself to enjoy the feel of him. His warmth. His solidness. Cash's heart pounded in his chest, a familiar rhythm that usually played after their intense lovemaking.

Before memories spiraled her too deep to claw her way out, she pushed away from his hold. Stumbling backwards, she jabbed her finger toward the door. "Leave, Cash. Go!"

"No," he said. "Baby, I can't lose you. I—" His words caught. "—can't lose you. I love you."

Finley shrugged. "How, Cash? How can you love me, yet hurt me like this? How can you love the woman you blame for your sister's death? How can I ever be comfortable knowing that when you look at me..." Her words trailed. Why was she wasting her energy? There was only one thing left to say to him. "It's over, Cash."

Something inside her broke the second the words floated past her lips. But what kind of future could they have together?

Cash didn't say another word. He stared at her for a long moment, turned, and moved to the door. But instead of leaving through it, he closed it. Why the hell was he making this so hard?

"Cash—"

"Just listen, Finley. Please," he said over his

shoulder.

His voice was strained when he spoke, void of the confidence that usually lingered there. It didn't take much to see he was hurting, but so was she.

"The night of the accident…" After a long pause, he continued, "The night of the accident, Chandler and I'd had another huge argument about the wedding. Something petty as usual. Instead of dealing with it, I left." He finally turned to face her. "The weather outside that night was treacherous. Wind. Rain. Thunderstorm. No one should have been out in those conditions."

Finley wasn't sure where this was leading, but she held to his every word.

"I wish like hell I would have had sense enough to stay home. Had my actions been different, the outcome would have been different. I don't blame you for Jaicee's death, Finley, I blame myself. Always have."

Finley wanted to tell him that it was no one's fault. That Jaicee hydroplaning and crashing had been a tragic accident. She also wanted to offer that had he not been out that night, a mother and her kids would have perished. But she remained silent.

"When you told me you'd ignored her call that night…" He shook his head. "I guess I needed someone else to help shoulder the blame that I have carried for so long. You didn't deserve that."

Damn right she didn't. Pain lingered in Cash's eyes and Finley could hear it in his words as well as feel it in his energy. All of this was clearly hard for him to talk about.

"God knows I never meant to hurt you, Finley, and I hope one day you can forgive me." His hand on the doorknob, he said, "For the record, the *only* thing I see when I look at you is the woman who brought me back to life."

Finley tried her best to downplay how much the statement had touched her, but failed miserably. Why couldn't she simply ignore her heart and think with her head?

"And regardless of what you think, I do love you, and I would never use those words as a ploy. I love you from the depths of my soul and nothing will ever change that."

Finley silenced her pleading heart.

He started to leave but stopped again. "I'm not giving up on us. I'll be back tomorrow, the day after that, and the day after that."

That was stalking, she wanted to say.

"I'll keep coming back until I can stand before you and not see your love for me dancing in your eyes. I know you love me,

Finley, because the taste of your love still lingers in my mouth."

*

Cash hadn't gotten but halfway out Finley's front door when he heard her soft voice. Saying a quick thank you to whatever entity that'd had pity on him, he stepped back inside. He didn't get his hopes too high, but if she was talking, that had to be a good sign.

"The reason I didn't take Jaicee's call that night was because she could always read me like a book." When Cash stepped back inside, she continued. "I was too ashamed to have to tell her that Joseph had gotten angry and left me in a restaurant parking lot in the pouring rain and with no way home. I walked away from him that night and never looked back."

Cash ground his teeth so hard it hurt. The idea of anyone doing that to Finley filled him with rage. "I'm sorry that happened to you," he said.

"I always seem to end up on the wrong side of love," she said.

Cash rested his hand on the backside of her neck. When she didn't pull away, he felt a wash of relief. "Not this time."

"I want to believe you, but—"

"Believe *in* me, Finley. Believe that I love you more than life. And forgive me, baby. Forgive me. Please forgive me."

Seizing the opportunity, he captured her mouth in a heady kiss. Feeling her lips against his again felt like sunshine on an icy day. Nothing had ever tasted so sweet. When she melted against him, he deepened the kiss, allowing his tongue to gobble her up.

After what seemed like an eternity, he ended the kiss, cradled her face between his hand, and stared deep into her eyes. "No buts. Let me love you like no man has ever dared to love you before." He kissed the corner of her mouth. "Give me your heart, Finley, and I swear I'll take great care of it. I'll show up every single day for you, for us."

There it was. He'd put his heart on the line again. All he could do was wait to see if Finley reeled it in. Her gaze locked to his. He swore she was looking past his eyes and into his soul. Was she looking for the love he'd claimed lingered there for her? The longer she remained silent, the more apprehensive he became. When he couldn't take it another second, he said, "Say something, please."

Another intense second or two passed before Finley spoke. "I forgive you and I know you love me." She rested a warm hand on the side of his face. "And I love you, too, Cassius Jabar Warren."

And he would make damn sure she always would.

Epilogue
One year later...

Finley waddled into Pleasure Pastries, because at eight months pregnant and as wide as a food truck, you no longer simply walked anywhere. She rubbed tiny circles over her protruding belly when her little one started to kick. Clearly, he or she knew they were about to get a treat.

She joined her father-in-law and Cash's uncle at their booth. Standing there, she sighed, "You two have a remedy for everything, whatcha got for inducing labor. This little tike has baked long enough," she said.

Uncle Rudolph didn't hesitate with his answer. "Sex. A lot of sex. I read it in a magazine."

His response didn't surprise her. He was the horniest old man she knew.

"Ignore him," her father-in-law said.

"May I?" he asked, hovering a hand above her belly.

When she nodded, a wide smile bloomed on his face.

"My grandson—"

"*Or* granddaughter," Finley corrected as she always did.

"—or granddaughter, will come when it's

time. There's no need to rush. Although, I'll be dang happy when he, or *she*, makes an appearance."

So would she. "I didn't see the food truck outside, is my handsome husband here?" Finley asked.

She and Cash had married exactly eight months ago today in an intimate ceremony overlooking the Blue Ridge Mountains. They'd spent the first leg of their honeymoon at The Grove Park Inn and had road-tripped the second half. Hitting all the spots they had during their first road trip and adding a few more.

When she playfully scolded him about getting her pregnant on their honeymoon, he'd told her not to worry because he planned to get her pregnant again on their first anniversary to balance things out. She hadn't exactly balked at the idea. They wanted a huge family together.

"He's in the back. Romeo is operating the food truck today," her father-in-law said.

Pleasure Pastries had become one of Raleigh's premier eateries. Cash had added a number of new items to the menu, including more lunch options and now offered dinner selections. They were on track to open three new locations by next year, including one in Asheville as well as Chicago, since both locations meant so much to them.

As for her company, it was doing quite well. Mr. Kilmer ended his relationship with The M. VanBeran Agency and had eagerly signed a contract with The Mountain View Agency, several of Madison's other clients had followed suit.

Life was good.

Cash appeared from the kitchen, "Pop, every time I turn around, you're feeling up my wife. I'm gonna have to keep an eye on you."

Eldridge's head pointed to Rudolph. "He's the one you gotta look out for."

Uncle Rudolph made a scoffing sound. "I don't touch pregnant women. I might jinx myself."

They all laughed.

Sobering, Cash kissed Finley on the cheek, keeping it G-rated in front of the two elders. "Hey, baby," he said.

The man still made her heart flutter when he called her baby. "Hey yourself."

Kneeling in front of her, he rested his hands and forehead on her stomach. "And hey baby."

Their child responded to the sound of his voice, moving around as if super excited to hear him. Finley understood completely.

After kissing her stomach, Cash returned to a full stand. "How are you feeling?"

"Like a walrus, but thank you for asking."

"You're the most beautiful walrus I've ever seen," Cash said lovingly.

"Uh-oh," Uncle Rudolph mumbled.

"Uh-oh, what?" Cash said.

Finley swatted Cash playfully. "Did you just call me a walrus?" she asked.

A quizzical expression spread across Cash's face. "Huh? I… You… No?" It sounded more like a question than an answer. "Help me out here," he said, turning to his father and uncle, who both tossed up their hands as if to say, *you're on your own with this one.* "Do you want a muffin?" Cash asked.

Displaying faux anger, she said, "Of course I want a muffin." It worked every time. What could she say? She was eating for two. Leading the way into the kitchen, she said, "All I know is this baby needs to come soon."

Pulling her into a storage closet and closing the door, Cash gave her a kiss so powerful she was convinced it got her a little closer to labor. He was still the best kisser she'd ever known, best man she'd ever known, and no doubt will be the best father she'd ever known.

"God, I love you Finley Rosette Warren. More and more each second."

"I love you, too, Cassius Jabar Warren. Always have, always will."

Three weeks later, they welcomed Claymont Jaycee Warren into the world.

THE END

ABOUT THE AUTHOR

By day, Joy Avery works as a customer service assistant. By night, the North Carolina native travels to imaginary worlds –creating characters whose romantic journeys invariably end happily ever after.

Since she was a young girl growing up in Garner, Joy knew she wanted to write. Stumbling onto romance novels, she discovered her passion for love stories. Instantly, she knew these were the type stories she wanted to pen.

Real characters. Real journeys. Real good love is what you'll find in a Joy Avery romance.

Joy is married with one child. When not writing, she spends her time playing with glitter.

OTHER BOOKS BY JOY AVERY

Indigo Falls
His Until Sunrise (Book 1)
His Ultimate Desire (Book 2)

The Lassiter Sisters
Never (Book 1)
Maybe (Book 2)
Always (Book 3)

The Cardinal House (Kimani Romance)
Soaring on Love (Book 1)
Campaign for His Heart (Book 2)
The Sweet Taste of Seduction (Book 3
Written with Love (Book 4)

Kimani Romance
In the Market for Love

Standalone Titles
Smoke in the Citi
Cupid's Error
One Delight Night
A Gentleman's Agreement
The Night Before Christian
Another Man's Treasure

Anthology Titles
A Bid on Forever (Distinguished Gentlemen series)

WHERE YOU CAN FIND JOY

WWW.JOYAVERY.COM
FACEBOOK.COM/AUTHORJOYAVERY
TWITTER.COM/AUTHORJOYAVERY
PINTEREST.COM/AUTHORJOYAVERY
AUTHORJOYAVERY@GMAIL.COM

Visit Joy's website to sign up for the
Wings of Love Newsletter

Be sure to follow me on:
AMAZON
BOOKBUB

Made in the USA
Monee, IL
18 June 2020

33440059R00083